BLUE SUMMER

A Novel

Other fiction books by Islandport Press

Closer All the Time
by Jim Nichols

This Time Might Be Different
by Elaine Ford

Contentment Cove
by Miriam Colwell

Pink Chimneys, Abbott's Reach, and *The Havener Sisters*
by Ardeana Hamlin

Random Act
by Gerry Boyle

Stealing History, Breaking Ground, and *Mapping Murder*
by William D. Andrews

Strangers on the Beach
by Josh Pahigian

The Contest
by James Hurley

These and other books are available at:
www.islandportpress.com

BLUE SUMMER

A Novel

JIM NICHOLS

ISLANDPORT PRESS

ISLANDPORT PRESS

Islandport Press
P.O. Box 10
Yarmouth, Maine 04096
www.islandportpress.com
info@islandportpress.com

First Islandport Edition / August 2020

ISBN: 978-1-952143-03-8
ebook ISBN: 978-1-952143-06-9
LCCN: 2020932368

Publisher: Dean Lunt
Book Design: Teresa Lagrange, Islandport Press
Cover image courtesy of iStock.com/chainatp
Printed in the USA

For Anne

"In the blue summer evenings, I will go along the paths . . . "
—Arthur Rimbaud

Bolduc Correctional Facility, 1997

So I thought I'd try to write this down. Chances are I'm no literary savant, but I promise my heart's in the right place, and I *have* been a world-class bookworm for my whole pathetic life, so maybe that'll help. Who knows? I guess we'll see. I think it's worth telling, at any rate, and I don't see anyone else volunteering to do it. And Lord knows I've got plenty of time now to try and figure it out, thanks to the Great State of Maine.

My name is Calvin Shaw. No household name, to be sure, but I wouldn't be surprised if it still rang a bell with some of you out there. There were some pretty lurid headlines at the time, after all: *Musician Kills Stepfather with Trumpet*, that sort of thing.

I can hear you now: You're *that* guy!

Yep, I'm that guy. But you might also have heard of me if you're into cool jazz. I'll bet you're at least familiar with some of my music. "Blue Summer," for instance. Everybody knows "Blue Summer" because Tony Bennett had a hit with it (after a lyricist named Billy Weber added words to my music), and any number of artists have covered it since.

It was a long, blue summer, the wrong blue summer . . .

And so on. You remember. And maybe Weber's words weren't exactly what I had in mind, but I'm not complaining. I'm lucky the thing exists at all—never mind becoming a near-standard, if I do say so myself—because there were some pretty long odds against that

1

happening, reason being that it chose such a dismal time in my life to come dancing along.

See, I'd about decided to bring the old curtain down.

I'm not exactly sure why it had come to that. I mean, I'd been a recent guest of the Pinellas County Jail, which wasn't what you'd call a real morale booster, and I was also drying out, which can do funny things to your head. But I'd been way low-down before without thinking it might be time to jump off a bridge.

It doesn't matter anyway. It's just that that's where things stood when this stubborn little melody showed up, and that's a big part of my story: that I was at a low point, maybe a bottom, and then "Blue Summer" came along and started to turn things around.

TIN PARADISE

ONE

Tampa, 1995

We'll start at that low point: a trailer park in Tampa, Florida. It's early in the morning, still dark outside, and the phone has startled me awake. I'm lying on my little fold-out bed waiting for it to stop. I'm not in the greatest of moods, because good sleep has been hard to come by. For once I was there, and now someone's trying to ruin it. The longer the phone rings, the more pissed off I get, and in no time I want to rip it out of the wall and smash it on the floor.

But then I remember what I've pretty much decided.

I remember that it likely makes no real difference anymore how much sleep I get, or whether I drag my sorry ass out of bed and answer the phone. None of it matters, because it's become only a matter of time. (Which isn't to say that I have to be in any big hurry, either. It's like deciding to rob a bank: just because you've made up your mind doesn't mean you have to run right out and buy a ski mask, right?)

So I take a deep breath and let the irritation bleed off. And when the ringing finally stops I stretch out and let my arms fall back. I feel the indifferent old world reconstruct itself around me. It's the same world as yesterday: I'm alone in a trailer park, and pretty soon I'll smell empanadas and coffee, and I'll hear radios playing, and maybe a rough-running car or two warming up.

I can already hear traffic on Dearborne Street.

There's always traffic on Dearborne, and there's always somebody blowing his horn. Like the guy I hear now, really leaning on it, running on down the road.

When he's gone I wonder if that blast was meant for anyone in particular. It's easy to imagine some other poor soul lying awake, listening. Maybe like me: pushing middle age, stretched out in their skivvies under a dingy old army surplus blanket in a beat-up old trailer. But not *exactly* like me, unless there's a brand-new melody playing *sotto voce* in his head.

You remember about the melody, right? Well, this is exactly when it arrives, slipping in as if to fill the vacuum left by my unconsummated little fit of anger about the phone.

At first it's barely present, like a leftover piece of dream. It doesn't flicker and fade, though, and then it takes on enough shape that I can hear it clearly. There's an intricate run of pure-sounding notes. It's different and interesting, a bit gloomy, and my right foot starts to slowly tap, and the next thing I know, a piece of lyric joins the party, which for me always means things are moving along. (The words themselves aren't important. Most of them won't even survive. They're just place-holders, rhythm-makers.)

They drive fast and blow their horns a lot on Dearborne.

That's what plays in my head, but it changes almost immediately into something better: *They speed and honk their horns a lot in Tampa.*

I ponder that melody and rhythm for a few minutes.

But thinking about traffic reminds me suddenly of counting cars on the River Road with my sister Julie and her best friend Becky O'Dell (who was red-haired and nice, but who lurched when she walked for no good reason; more on that later), and all at once it's not about Dearborne or Tampa at all anymore.

Now it's about Julie and me, about our brother Alvin (yeah, Calvin and Alvin—it wasn't my idea) and my parents and Becky and that POS Randy Pike and everybody else connected to where I grew up in Baxter, Maine; which means it's also about all the tragedy that started during that bluest of summers. (Which I'll get to, but for now, back to the trailer.)

I tap out the rhythm against my chest, and then whistle it softly, on the intake (to be quiet), and to fix it in my mind I snap open the beat-up cornet case that's always on the floor nearby. I want to feel what it's like to play it. I take out this sweet little Olds that I picked up in a pawnshop in NYC, touch the smooth mother-of-pearl caps and flutter the valves, liking the silky action and the *plupetty-plup* sound that I always imagine is a soft little musical engine trying to start.

I mute the horn with my hand and tease my new tune out, and I mark that it's coming out in D minor, which suits its rather serious and melancholy feeling.

After a bit I walk down to my little tin box of a bathroom, still playing, and I stop long enough to do my business and then, coming back, I try and draw the melody out a little more, hoping to coax it into something that might resolve.

It's still not a huge deal, but it's gaining weight. I'm playing around, almost out of habit, but at the same time getting more involved, even becoming a little wary about where it might be going, what it might have to say about my family, and especially, my father and Julie.

See, it's taking me somewhere I wasn't expecting.

Which happens sometimes: You have a direction in mind and you're trying to fulfill it, and you're rolling along fine, and then there's an association of some kind and a change of direction, maybe darker, and you're pulled down another path. (Which isn't different from life itself, now that I think about it—at least, my messed-up life.)

Anyway, I sit back down on the bed and fiddle until I'm pretty sure it's not going to show itself entirely at this moment—it's holding back, as if the time isn't right—and then I'm all the way awake, so I put the cornet away and go into my little tin box of a kitchen and pour myself a heaping bowl of Cheerios.

I turn on the box radio for the traffic report. This is routine, because I've been driving taxi, which is what I do when music gigs are hard to come by, which they have been lately. People get out of the habit of thinking of you when you go to jail, even if it's only for a couple of months. I haven't exactly been out there knocking on doors since I was released, either.

The traffic reporter is talking about a slowdown caused by an overturned potato truck. I chew the cereal and wonder what a potato truck was doing in Tampa, Florida. For all I know they drive potatoes down here all the time, but it's odd, because I've just been thinking about Maine.

Then I think, For all I know, they're Idaho spuds.

Anyway, the reporter goes on about cars skidding on the squashed potatoes. His voice is shaky. He guesses it'll be mid-morning before traffic is back to normal, which means all the usual routes into town will be clogged.

I say, "Well, fuck the mother-fucking duck," as if that traffic report actually matters, and snap the radio off. (I got that catchy little phrase from my Pinellas cellmate, Rocky Kincaid, who was a decent sax man, known as Skinny-Ass One around the yard. I was Skinny-Ass Two, but I've put on a few pounds since I got out. Our stays had overlapped for close to thirty days—me, for what they called *Disorderly Intoxication* plus *Assault on a Police Officer*, Rocky, for *Attempting to Purchase a Controlled Substance*).

I put my bowl in the sink, yank open the sticky door, and go outside for a Lucky Strike. It's my first of the day, which always makes me feel guilty, but you can't give up everything. (I quit drinking when I went to jail, and that's an accomplishment I don't want to ruin, even if it wasn't of my own volition, but I don't feel that way about smoking.)

Not that any of it matters, I remind myself.

I sit on the stoop, looking around the trailer park. It's not quite dawn, warm and humid already. Cars and trucks are running by on Dearborne and nighthawks are blowing their horns. I can see the traffic light flashing red (the only light around, because all the streetlights have been busted out).

There are little birds chirping from the bushes behind me.

The phone rings again, and I don't move. I cross my ankles and smoke with no hands. The ash falls on my shirt and I brush it off. Maybe it's somebody with a gig, but I don't really care. I can take it or leave it, now.

After a while the ringing stops. I scratch my stubble and wait for my ride to show. Yeah, I'm still going to work. I thought about quitting, but it makes more sense to have a few bucks coming in while I'm playing out the string. Giving up seems to have lifted my spirits in some contrary way, and I figure I might as well enjoy it while I can.

Which is a perfect mood for what happens next.

I've just lit a second cigarette off the stub of the first and I'm watching the red sun edge up over the horizon when the door of this rattletrap trailer across the lane pops open and these three little urchins come out and stand on the step.

Tampa, 1995

I've gotten to know two of these kids. They're brother and sister, and always a little shy at first. Their heads are down and they're looking sideways at each other. The third kid—a boy—is looking doubtfully at me, waiting to see about the beat-up white dude across the way. They're all still in their PJs.

After I say "You all can come on over if you want," it still takes a few seconds, but then they're standing in front of me, looking down at the dirt.

"Bet I can guess what you want," I say. "Huh, Carlo?"

"Uh-huh," says one of the boys.

"Can't you look at me?"

Carlo's bright eyes flicker up.

"You too, Ava," I say.

Ava looks up for a millisecond, then ducks her head again. She's as pretty as Carlo is handsome, and being a little girl, she's extra special to me.

"And what's your friend's name?"

"Joaquin." Carlo makes a face. "You like that name?"

"Sure, that's a fine name."

"He live over there." Carlo flings an arm out toward the far end of the trailer park, where the orange pickers live, facing a row of slatted privies across a muddy ditch.

"Well," I say, "we all gotta live somewhere."

Joaquin frowns.

"So," I say. "Magic trick?"

"Invisible ball!" Carlo says.

Ava moves a little closer.

"I don't have a paper bag," I say.

Carlo brings one out from behind his back.

"I don't know, man. I don't know if my magic works on old wrinkled-up lunch bags."

"Aw, man . . ." Carlo says.

"We can give it a try, though."

I stick a hand in the bag.

Carlo nudges Joaquin, who slaps at his arm.

I pluck something out of thin air, pretend to pop it into my mouth. Then I move my tongue around from cheek to cheek.

"That is just his tongue!"

"You wait!" Carlo says.

I take the invisible ball out of my mouth, walk away from the stoop and toss it underhanded into the air. I hold the paper bag out and snap my thumb against the bottom of the bag.

"See!" Carlo says.

"Do it again!" Joaquin says.

I let the ball spill out into my palm, toss it up again, and step to the side.

Snap!

Carlo does a little scuff step, claps his hands.

Ava holds her breath.

I throw the ball higher, circling under it like a catcher after a pop-up, and catch it again in the wrinkly old lunch bag.

The kids clap their hands and it makes me laugh. I could do this all day. But then a horn blasts out on Dearborne, and a taxi comes whistling around the corner. There's a trail of dust behind it and a man with a bushy, gray beard at its wheel. The kids shriek in mock terror—they've seen this guy before—and fly back across the lane. The door of their trailer clatters shut as the taxi pulls up.

I crumple the paper bag and toss it into my trailer. Then I lock the door and walk through the dust to the car. The driver grins at me as I slide into the front seat.

"Playing with the porch monkeys again?"

"Don't be an asshole, Neal." I know he's a dumbass who doesn't know any better, but it always riles me when someone's not cool with kids.

He laughs, spins the steering wheel, looks backwards, his beard pooling up on the shoulder of his ratty green field jacket. Then he pulls a U-turn in front of the kids' trailer. He has his ignition key on a big ring with other keys and a metal swastika-shaped bottle opener. He's a burly guy who always steers his cab with both hands.

"They shit on us too." As if that makes it right.

"Not those little kids."

"Wait until they grow up."

"If they do, brother, you asked for it."

Neal wrangles us through the intersection and onto Dearborne, cutting off a pickup truck. The pickup's horn blares as it rushes by, and we both—cabbies, right?—casually flip him off.

He steps on the gas toward the airport. There's a railroad berm on our left with some kind of sunburnt hedge in front of the rails, and scruffy countryside on our right, sloping down a long way to the orange groves. The sky is getting lighter. Far ahead I can see the Tampa skyline.

Neal pulls into the left lane, blows past someone on a straightaway and cuts back in quick. They honk at us, too, a double honk, and my mind takes a quick leap from that onto my new melody.

It's been with me the whole morning, very persistent but still not complete, and I'm starting to have this feeling that it wants me to stick around for its own sake, and that's why it's holding back, trying to make itself irresistible. I snicker under my breath at the idea: a piece of music choosing me at this stage of my life. That would take a stronger belief in the whole idea of fate, or destiny, than I possess (and would also negate the random aspect of direction and change that I was thinking about earlier, wouldn't it?).

But as we ride along toward Tampa, the melody teasing me, I let myself go there. What have I got to lose, right? And I wonder: What if it's important? What if I happen to be the rickety gateway it needs, for whatever reason? What if it needs me like *Starry Night* needed van Gogh and "Julia" needed John Lennon? I'm not equating myself, but I don't have to: some amazing work has come from lesser mortals.

Think one-hit wonders like "Sweet Lorraine" and "Undecided."

Neal shifts in his seat and I look at him steering with his knees while he sticks a pinch of snuff up under his lip. We're still going eighty-five. He looks back and offers the tin, but I shake my head because I'd rather get his hands back on the wheel. He shrugs and stuffs the tin back into one of his many pockets.

Finally his hands go back where they belong.

I look out the window at the low countryside and ponder my fantasized role in bringing this new melody into the world, and I think, what the hell, go ahead and snicker. Maybe it's a flight of fancy, but if the tune keeps after me, and convinces me I need to stick around, and I decide I have to postpone the other thing, then what the hell?

I can try my best and see what happens, and when the time comes, still do what I have to do.

Win-win, right?

So I watch the city ahead of us glow with the sunrise, and I tell myself it's not that bad to be going to work and thinking about new music and feeling halfway decent. Maybe I should just enjoy it while it lasts. Because if there's anything I've learned during my thirty-odd years of the blues, it's just how evanescent these decent moments can be.

PREHISTORIC

THREE

Baxter, Summer, 1964

So, we're talking thirty years. That takes me back to age ten, which is when everything started to go sideways. The Fourth of July that year, to be precise, although the day itself started out all right.

When I rolled out of my bunk and headed downstairs for breakfast we were a normal, small-town family—mom, dad, three kids—with no real worries about anything. We lived where Shaws had always lived, except for a few years after my grandparents moved to Bath during the war, so my grandfather could work in the shipyard.

We went to church like everybody else. We sat down to supper together and my father asked us questions about our day. We were expected to answer thoughtfully; he was the boss. We had chores to do and music lessons to practice—my father believed firmly that music lessons were a necessity—and we were supposed to mind what he and my mother said.

My father, John Shaw—known as Jack—was a former high school sports hero and current town selectman, a man who'd survived several battles in the Pacific Theater during World War II, who still wore the St. Christopher medal my grandmother gave him when he left for boot camp. After coming home he'd parlayed his veteran status and all-around good name into a decent living selling cars at the local GM dealership, and as a result, we were fairly comfortably middle-class.

My mom, Betty Flint Shaw, grew up in Palo Alto, but was pretty and smart enough to mostly overcome that handicap with her Maine neighbors, although there were some reservations because she wasn't all that friendly, and had never learned how to small-talk. In fact, she was something of a cold fish even with us. But that wasn't her fault, according to my father. When I wondered one day why she wasn't as friendly as my friend's mother, he said, "Well, your mother has never quite figured that kind of thing out." And when I said "Why not?" he said, "You'd have to ask her parents." I must have looked unsatisfied, because he grinned and tousled my hair. "None of us is perfect, right, Old Cal? Besides, you can't say she doesn't try." And it was true; on rare and unexpected occasions she would plant a kiss on your cheek or reach an arm around you and attempt a tender squeeze.

Anyway, it was the Fourth, and after breakfast we piled into the station wagon and went to the parade. There were fire engines and floats, Boy Scouts and Little Leaguers, veterans and politicians. The downtown was hung with red, white and blue bunting, and there was a balloon vendor with a helium tank. People had their dogs on leashes, and kids were jumping out from behind telephone poles with squirt guns.

The parade took an hour. The last float—Betsy Ross with an American flag on her lap—went by, followed by a dozen vets, including my father and Uncle Gus (who wasn't really an uncle), marching with their arms swinging, and a half-dozen Red Cross nurses, including my mother (who'd trained as a nurse's assistant but had never deployed, because the war had ended).

We kids trailed them to the town hall, where everyone broke ranks and made for the park behind the Main Street block, which had been set up for a chicken barbecue, with a giant grill and a dozen long tables under an awning.

I ate the chicken, the coleslaw, the potato chips, and the brownie, everything except the pickle, which my faux uncle Gus Shaw "liberated" from my plate with a fat-fingered flourish (think Chris Farley putting on airs).

It was hot, but nobody bothered with sunblock. Red cheeks and arms were part of the deal. Out past the tables there were horseshoe and wood-splitting contests, pony rides and face-painting, and more balloons. Over near Baxter Elementary School some girls had set up a card table with a record player and were playing Beatles records and doing the twist. (The Beatles were a new thing in Maine that year. So was the twist, for that matter.)

After we ate my father lit his pipe, joined the line for horseshoes, put his hands on his hips, and said, "Well, I don't see any competition to worry about here."

The other men laughed and insulted him back.

My mother and Uncle Gus stayed to watch, and we kids were turned loose for an hour, after which we were instructed to meet at the fire station.

My father told us to try and pretend we were civilized.

Alvin and I galloped off, while Julie—a newly fledged teenager—walked with dignity toward the music. Her friend Becky O'Dell broke out of a crowd of kids to join her, and they went the rest of the way together, Julie in her new summer dress, Becky in her usual overalls, hobbling efficiently to keep up. (She was an odd case in that—as I mentioned before—there was nothing congenitally wrong with her legs. It was just that when she was a toddler she'd learned to walk by imitating her older brother, who had cerebral palsy, and her parents, who thought it was cute, had let it go on until she was stuck that way.)

If I remember right, Julie was a Paul girl; Becky loved Ringo. I didn't like any of them at first—out of jealousy, I guess.

Anyway, Alvin and I took off the other way and joined a couple of schoolmates, the four of us pretending to be tough guys, pushing and shoving one another, sassing grown-ups and trading insults with a cluster of teenage hoods until they ran us off by snapping their cigarettes away and feinting toward us.

It was, of course, over too quickly. I knew the hour was up when Alvin raised the new Timex on his wrist, took a couple of steps backward with his eyes on me and then spun and ran off for the fire station.

"Hey!" I ditched our friends and sprinted after him.

Alvin ran like some kind of bird, jabbing his feet and jutting his chin, but he had long legs and was pretty fast. I'd still have caught him, though, if there hadn't been so many people in the way, or if it had been a little farther.

"Beat you!" he gasped, when we'd windmilled to a stop.

"You jumped the gun."

"No sir," Alvin said, still panting.

"Here's Julie," our mother said.

She came strolling up and Uncle Gus clicked his heels and saluted our father.

"All stragglers present and accounted for, sir. What should we do with them, sir?"

He liked to play up that Dad had outranked him in the service, but it was also funny because of his pudginess and the slightly wet way that he talked.

"Throw 'em in the brig!"

"Aye aye, sir!"

We walked back through town—slowly, because it seemed like everyone we met wanted to shake Dad's hand and chat. We turned down School Street to where we'd left the station wagon parked next to a row of school buses.

Driving home it was steaming in the car, and we rolled down the windows and let the warm air blow in. Above us the sky was deep blue with big, billowy clouds, and a breeze off the river made the tops of the pines sway. Once that Dodge got up to speed it could really go, and we rumbled past woods and open fields and fenced-in old farmhouses with teetering barns and fat silos. I caught glimpses of the water, which looked sluggish because the tide was just changing.

Alvin and I sprawled in the way-back, where we could feel every bump. A big one would sometimes lift us right off the deck, and make us laugh and groan after we landed.

Julie sat beside Uncle Gus, reading an Andre Norton paperback she'd found on the floor. (Our father planted books—and a pipe— anywhere that he might find himself with time on his hands: the bathroom, the car, his boat.)

Our mother was in the front seat, watching the scenery.

After a while Alvin and I started bickering about dinosaurs. We'd been fighting over them for a month, since my father had asked me a crossword question about the Mesozoic without giving my older brother first crack at it.

It made sense to ask me, because I was the one with dinosaur books all over the house, but to my older brother it was a serious breach of family protocol. And it didn't help when I came up with the answer and my father said, "Good man!"

Afterward Alvin dived right into one of those books, a big hardcover called *Prehistoric Animals* that I'd gotten for Christmas. I caught him curled up with it on the porch swing and knew immediately what he was up to. He was a quick study, so it was only a day or two until he was ready to chime in on the subject, and he'd been looking for openings ever since. Today he'd started in while we were crossing the bridge over the Baxter River.

"This area would have been crawling with Diplodocuses in prehistoric times," he'd announced, which had compelled me to say something equally loud about how they actually preferred marshes and swamps.

Which was all it took. We went back and forth about the Diplodocus, and before long were arguing over whether my favorite— *Tyrannosaurus rex*—would have been annihilated in a fight with Allosaurus.

"Ridiculous! Tyrannosaurus was way bigger."

"But Allosaurus was a much better fighter."

"You're full of it!"

"Don't be childish," he said, which was one of his favorite gambits: pretending to be the grown-up after he'd started the whole thing. (He desperately *wanted* to be a grown-up, and wore chinos and collared jerseys that he buttoned up to his neck, while I was dungarees and T-shirts.)

I kissed the tip of my middle finger.

"Cal just gave me the finger!" he yelled.

Our mother turned in her seat and shot us a look.

"I was just biting my fingernail."

"You're a liar!"

"That's enough." She stared until we looked away, then faced front again. Our mother had little tolerance for tomfoolery (which was another thing that could make her unlikable.)

Alvin sneered at me. I shifted sideways, managing to kick his leg in the process. It wasn't much more than a nudge, but he squealed anyway, and our mother yanked herself back around.

"I'm warning you two."

Uncle Gus, sitting in the line of fire, cleared his throat. He hated discord. Julie just kept reading. Our father wasn't paying any attention; he was whistling under his breath, his elbow out the window, other hand on the wheel, mind somewhere else.

"But he kicked me!" Alvin whined.

"I barely touched the little baby."

He jabbed a foot out. "How do you like it?"

I took a swipe back at him and then we were grunting and wrestling in the small space.

"John!" our mother demanded.

Our father started, looked wide-eyed at her, and pulled the car over to the shoulder. We felt it as we slowed down and separated before he threw the gearshift into park.

He turned in the seat and looked at us.

"Do I have to come back there?"

"No, sir," we said.

"Then knock it off." He held his gaze until I muttered, "Sorry." Then he raised an eyebrow at our mother, checked for traffic, and drove us back into the southbound lane.

Alvin and I glowered, but kept our hands to ourselves.

Our father went back to daydreaming about his aircraft carrier during the war, maybe, or some even-par stretch at the Baxter Golf Club, or fly-fishing at Whetstone Falls on the East Branch of the Penobscot River, which he claimed as his favorite place on Earth.

Our mother kept turning abruptly to look preemptively at us, which made it hard for our father to keep daydreaming, and after a while I could see he was looking at us too in the rearview mirror. And since he could never be aware of us without his boyish side coming out, it wasn't long until he said, "You know, this wouldn't be a bad day for a game of croquet."

Alvin and I cheered from the way-back. Julie lowered her book. Uncle Gus grinned, and even our mother managed a smile. We'd only learned about croquet that summer.

"I only wish I could find some decent competition." Our father cocked his head mock-sadly toward our mother, who rolled her eyes.

"You can!" Alvin shouted.

"Yeah," I said, "me!"

"I've heard that sad song before." He winked at the mirror. "Now Julie might give me a run for my money, if we could only keep her away from the booze."

Julie looked up at the mirror and they smiled at each other.

"Look out!" our mother cried then.

A tractor pulling a hay wagon had just come rocking around a curve, hogging the middle of the road. Our father had to yank the Dodge close to the shoulder to avoid being sideswiped. Then the hay wagon was behind us, swaying along toward town, and we were all able to breathe again.

"Will you please pay attention, John!"

"Saw him the whole time," our father said with a grin.

Our mother shook her head.

We crested a hill and started down the long slope that led to our house. At the bottom of the hill we passed our hayfield and then the old vegetable stand with its CLOSED sign hanging from a nail on one of the shutters. (The vegetable stand had come with the property. Sometimes Alvin and I used it for a clubhouse.)

We turned into the dirt driveway and rode past the barn—which was still partly red, but mostly weathered board—to our double-dormered farmhouse. Dad threw the gearshift and shut off the engine. All the side doors opened at once. I pulled the tailgate latch ahead of Alvin and scrambled out first.

Alvin slid out and gave me a shove, but I just laughed. I'd sprouted that spring and was almost as tall now, and I'd also gotten into some scraps at school—my growth had given me a sort of martial confidence on the playground—and acquitted myself quite well. So maybe he was still a year older but he didn't rule the roost the way he used to. (Which was probably another reason he'd been so touchy about the crossword question.)

"Save some of that energy," our father said.

We ran inside, and our parents changed out of their uniforms into shorts and jerseys. Uncle Gus didn't have a change of clothes, but took his jacket off and rolled up his sleeves.

There was a flat piece of lawn behind the barn, where the wickets and pegs had been set up since May, when the first truly warm weather had come in. Our father went into the barn for the rack that held the mallets and wooden balls. He carried it out with two hands at waist level and set it down near the home peg. We grabbed the mallets and balls: black for him, yellow for our mother, orange for Uncle Gus; blue, green and red for Julie, Alvin and me.

I tossed my red ball up and down in one hand, trying to make it look lighter than it was, while we drew straws to see who would go first. Our father won and took several practice swings, then wriggled like a golfer to set himself and somehow knocked his ball in a bumpy, erratic curve right through the first wicket.

"Heck of a shot!" Uncle Gus said, and clapped his hands.

"Nothing to it," our father said archly.

He won that first match going away, won another almost as easily, and then started to showboat, taking increasingly crazy shots and, when successful, imitating Cassius Clay, the new Heavyweight Champ, by holding his arms up and saying, "I am the greatest!" (Our father had boxed in the navy, and he'd loved it when Clay had put a beating on Sonny Liston that February.)

We all thought this was funny except Alvin, who was a chronic poor sport. He just got angry, and finally, when our father clinched one more victory by knocking Alvin's green ball clear off the playing field, he threw his mallet down, stomped over to the barn and sat on the old half-log bench by the side door, crossing his arms on his chest, eyes narrow and angry behind his thick-lensed glasses.

"Was that really necessary, John?"

My father shaded his eyes. "It's just part of the game."

"He's eleven years old."

Dad turned to look at Uncle Gus.

"Don't look at me!"

Our father rubbed his chin. "Well, I suppose we could call it a mulligan."

"Not fair!" I yelled, because I was now in second place.

"Shut up, Cal," Alvin said.

"You shut up."

And that was it for our mother, who wasn't competitive and had probably been looking for an excuse to quit. She said, "That's quite enough," picked up her yellow ball, and carried it away in the crook of her arm.

"Thanks for nothing!" Julie snapped at us.

"You're welcome." Alvin made a prissy face.

"Shut up!" She grabbed her own ball in two hands and set off after our mother, too angry to remember her new, stately walk. She could be feisty sometimes.

Our father looked at Uncle Gus, who held up his palms, and they started off, too—my father tall and broad-shouldered, Uncle Gus shorter and stout—with Alvin close behind, smirking over his shoulder.

I watched them go, and when they'd put their balls and mallets down and were on their way back to the house, I made a face at them and drove my red ball viciously toward the rack. There was a loud crack when it hit, but only Alvin looked back (with a sneer). Everybody else just kept moving.

I stomped over and kicked my ball the last few feet. Then I slammed it and the mallet into the rack. I didn't care anymore that nobody was paying attention. I was good and angry, and enjoying it enough that I let myself stay that way, right up until my father left after supper to play poker. Which is something I still feel guilty about, because it was the last chance I would ever have to be nice to him, and it would have been so easy, too.

FOUR

Baxter, Summer, 1964

After supper we watched *Wagon Train*, and when it was over our father said, "Well, I suppose," and got up from his recliner. He went around to where we kids sat on the green couch. "Don't let your mother rob any banks while I'm gone," he said, "or shoot any of the neighbors or anything. Okay? I'm counting on you, now."

Julie said "We won't!", but Alvin and I—still nursing our separate grievances—kept our mouths shut. We also ducked away when our father reached out to ruffle our hair.

"Tough guys, huh?" he said, and then he smiled and turned to kiss the top of my sister's head.

"Don't stay out all night," our mother said.

"It won't take me all night to clean out that crew."

"That's what you said last year."

He walked back to her, bent down and took her hand. He raised it and kissed her knuckles.

"And please don't drink too much."

"Wouldn't dream of it."

"You said that last year, too." She squinted up at him.

He grinned and waved to us on his way out of the living room. Only Julie waved back. When our mother heard the screen door shut, she rose from her chair and went into the kitchen. She'd changed out of her shorts and jersey into a pair of gray slacks and a green blouse.

I stretched myself over the arm of the couch to look down the hallway and saw her standing by the window. The window lit up when Dad's headlights hit it, and she seemed to tense. The light slid away and my mother cocked her head to keep it in sight. He was heading into town, going to the Amvets hall, which I knew sat on a low hill down a side street past the water tower.

Then he was gone and our mother stared for a moment longer before turning on the tap water and letting it run into the sink where the supper dishes sat.

I watched her for a few seconds more. But there was another Western coming on—*Gunsmoke*, maybe—and I hiked myself back into a sitting position. Soon I was lost in the action, and with my father gone, I finally forgot about being angry.

It gets difficult now, because this is where it all started to go bad. I didn't witness everything I'm going to describe. I saw some of it, and Uncle Gus told me a lot more a few years later, after I'd moved in with him. (We had a session at his kitchen table, drinking hard cider, where I pressed him for every detail of that night.)

Some I've had to imagine. It was necessary if I was going to tell it all, because my mother would never go there. But I'm pretty sure what I've conjured up is close to the truth. I knew everyone involved down to their toenails, after all.

Anyway, I'll do the best I can. I know, for example, that it was still dark when my mother opened her eyes that night to squint at the alarm clock on the side table, and I think we can assume it took a moment to realize that she was alone in bed in the middle of the night.

She must have come fully awake in a panic, then. I can picture her slipping into her robe and pulling the sash tight; I'd seen it a hundred times. And I actually did watch her pad out of their bedroom and go quietly downstairs, because I'd awakened, too—there was something in the air—and heard her door open, and when she came out I was lying on the floor in my doorway, chin in my hands.

She didn't see me, and after she'd gone halfway down the stairs I got up and followed. At the bottom I put my back to the wall and peered into the kitchen. She was looking out the window at the dark driveway.

She switched on the light above the sink—I crouched low to stay in the shadows—and walked over to the old rotary phone mounted on the wall next to the door. There would have been a click and a dial tone before she twirled in Uncle Gus's number, and then a hollow ring from the other end.

Uncle Gus told me it took a while to pick up, because he'd been sound asleep. "Hullo?" he said, and I'm pretty sure his voice was hoarse, because he chain-smoked and was always hoarse in the morning until he coughed up a certain amount of gunk.

"Gus?" my mother said.

"Betty? Is everything all right?"

"Jack never came home. What time did the game break up?"

"It was late," Uncle Gus said, "but he left before the rest of us. Said he was tired of taking our money and he was going to call it a night. Before midnight, I'm pretty sure."

"Well, he's not home."

Maybe here Uncle Gus cleared his throat again.

"I'm sure it's nothing. Give me a minute to throw some clothes on. I'll go and have a look. Most likely he just decided to pull over and take a nap."

"Did he drink a lot?"

"He had a few. I wouldn't say a lot."

"Can you pick me up? I can't sit here and wait."

Uncle Gus hesitated. "Okay, sit tight. I'll be right over."

My mother hung up, turned to go back upstairs, and stopped when she saw me in the doorway.

"What happened?" I said.

"Go back to bed, Cal."

"But where are you going?"

"Your father's broken down somewhere."

"I'll come with you."

"Your uncle is taking me. You go back to bed."

She followed me upstairs and waited until I grudgingly shut the door.

But I didn't go back to bed, and when she started back downstairs I cracked the door open to watch, and as soon as she turned into the kitchen I was on the move, avoiding the noisy stairs and hugging the wall. (I was a good sneak, with a lot of practice.)

Spying again from the kitchen doorway I saw her go outside. I hustled back through the living room to the side door and circled around the house to the north end of the porch. The grass was wet on my bare feet, and it was still warm, with a few stars behind the house but not eastward, past the river, where a band of pink had pushed over the tops of the pines.

Through the porch railing I saw her staring down the driveway. Her arms were crossed on her chest. We waited in the near-dark, together but separate.

Uncle Gus only lived a couple of miles away, but it seemed a long time until I heard him coming and then saw his headlights way up by the far curve. He didn't seem to be going nearly fast enough. Finally, though, he came down the long straightaway, headlights flickering through the tall trees, then disappearing behind the barn, finally emerging past the abandoned vegetable stand. He turned into our driveway, crunching over the gravel, came up past the barn, and stopped by the flagstoned walkway.

He shut the engine off, and I remember the quick silence and Mom waiting. Then he struggled bulkily out of the car and looked up at the house. When my mother realized he couldn't see her in the shadows, she moved onto the top step. He saw her then, put his hands in his pockets and looked down at his L.L.Bean boots.

Her heart must have begun to thump.

"He went off the road a mile or so back," Uncle Gus said to his boots. His voice sounded strangled, and as he stepped closer and looked at my mother, I could see that his face was beginning to fall in on itself.

"He didn't make it, Betty," he said, in the same squeezed voice. "I'm so sorry."

Then he came up the steps and put his arms around her. Her own arms stayed at her sides. While they stood there I ran back around the house, feeling as if I'd touched the electric fence at Talbot's dairy farm down the River Road across from Becky O'Dell's house. I made it upstairs before they came inside to call the police.

Before they left my mother came upstairs to tell us to go back to bed—Julie and Alvin were awake by this time, and had come out in their pajamas—and that she had to go with Uncle Gus, but she'd be back in a little while. She didn't sound like herself; her voice was shaky. She went back downstairs, and we stayed where we were.

"What's going on?" Julie asked me.

"Something happened to Daddy."

"What?"

"I'm not sure." (I wasn't sure exactly what awful thing Uncle Gus had meant by *He didn't make it.*) I went into my parents' bedroom and raised the window shade. Julie and Alvin followed me, and we watched Uncle Gus take our mother out to his car. He opened her door and waited until she was inside, then shut the door and walked heavily around to his side. It still wasn't quite dawn.

Uncle Gus told me later that he tried to talk her out of going at this point, but she wouldn't listen; she just sat there, waiting to leave. He started the engine, turned on the headlights, and drove back to the River Road. They rode along silently until he pulled onto the shoulder and shut off the engine. Then they looked at each other and he could tell they were both thinking the same thing: how awful that he'd been so close to home.

My mother was out before Uncle Gus could come around to her door, but had to stop and cover her mouth. Then she was moving again and he met her in front of the car. He took her arm and they walked across the damp road, past black tire marks that cut sharply toward the weedy ditch.

Lying in the ditch was a young spike-horn deer, midsection caved in, eyes glazed. They stepped past the carcass and came opposite a gap in the roadside brush.

It smelled like gasoline; they saw the Dodge overturned against a thick white pine. My mother pulled loose from Uncle Gus and stepped down into the ditch, hands out for balance. He followed, reaching, but she was already scrambling up the other side. He trailed her across the ripped ground and through the gap in the brush to the wagon.

The gasoline smell was stronger. My mother knelt and yanked at the buckled, inverted door, but it wouldn't budge. She pulled her jacket sleeve down and with the covered heel of her hand knocked chunks of glass out of the way, but she couldn't reach him because he was on the other side, upside down, knees to his chest. He was scrunched up like a kid, not a grown man, and his eyes were slightly open.

Uncle Gus told me later that he didn't look especially hurt. It was just his eyes. The other thing that stuck with him was the St. Christopher medal lying outside his shirt. ("I guess he used all the luck up during the war," he'd said, sitting at the kitchen table, and then he'd swiped at his eyes.)

"Oh, honey," Uncle Gus said now.

My mother turned and shoved her head and shoulders through the window, past jagged, flexible shards. He put his hands on her waist and carefully pulled her back, and walked her away from the car toward the road.

The ambulance came then, its siren growing louder until red light flashed on the treetops along the roadside. It stopped on the shoulder where the Dodge had sailed off the road, and two men jumped out and hurried past my mother and Uncle Gus to the station wagon.

The taller man dropped to his knees and shined his flashlight through the broken window. Almost at once the flashlight clicked off, and he straightened and turned away from the wrecked car.

Uncle Gus and my mother waited to hear that they'd been wrong, somehow. It was a last feeble hope, and they knew better because the tall man wouldn't be walking so sadly toward them, and besides, they'd seen Jack's eyes. But they held their breath anyway until the man said, "I'm so sorry, Mrs. Shaw."

My mother shut her eyes and turned her face into Uncle Gus's chest. Betty Flint Shaw never cried—had grown up tougher than that—and she didn't cry now. Not quite. But she held tightly to Uncle Gus and grieved. She was grieving for my father, of course, but I think that without knowing it she was also mourning that small, generally hidden tenderness that she had sensed trying to grow within her since she'd known him, and which was bound to sputter and die now that he was gone.

Baxter, Summer, 1964

Three days later we climbed the granite steps that led to the massive oak door of Sacred Heart Church. Uncle Gus held the door open. He wasn't a lot taller than my mother, but his round head seemed twice as large. He had on his old double-breasted navy dress uniform, and you could see the strain on the six gold buttons that held it shut.

He touched my mother's back as she went past him into the narthex, wearing a black dress to just below her knees, and a black jacket. I remember how her hair—lighter than mine or Alvin's, more like Julie's—had been sprayed stiff beneath her shallow black hat.

Behind her went Julie in her Sunday dress: dark blue with tiny white blossoms. Then Alvin and me in our too-small blazers, and next, my Shaw grandparents, who'd driven up from Bath. (It was the first time I'd seen them in two or three years; they weren't big on visiting.) Uncle Gus brought up the rear, holding his white cap in both hands.

The light inside the church had an odd tint because of tall, stained-glass windows. When we got to the first pew, my mother genuflected and stood aside while the rest of us filed past and sidestepped into place.

I looked at the monstrous coffin sitting in front of the altar. Its lid was open so that anyone who wanted could take a last look at John Shaw.

We'd said good-bye earlier, by ourselves. Julie and Alvin had gone first, then I'd put my hands on the heavy, dark wood and looked in at him. He was in dress uniform, his white hat on his chest, and he looked like my father: thick, dark hair, bushy eyebrows, cleft chin. I had the eerie feeling that he was only sleeping and might sit up at any moment.

It was strange, too, because you could never stare at him without his feeling it and looking around with a grin. Only this time, he just lay there, he didn't sit up or grin, and finally I made myself leave and walk stiffly back to the pew. My steps echoed in the open space of the church and left a dark resonance in my mind, a new feeling that added to the strangeness.

My grandparents took their turns, then finally my mother, bowing her head, making the sign of the cross. She looked in at him for a long moment, turned to come back, and I was shocked to see the hot, dark anger in her eyes. She was furious at him. She caught me looking and quickly hooded her eyes. Back in the pew she knelt briefly, sat back, and said, "All right, we can leave, now."

We walked out of the church and into the sunshine. I could smell the warm grass. There were people on the lawn, waiting to go in, chatting and smoking cigarettes and pipes. But this stopped when we appeared, and at the bottom of the steps they gathered to meet us.

Becky O'Dell waded up and hugged Julie. She put her cheek against Julie's and the breeze took her red hair and blew it around Julie's head. They stood that way until Becky's mother called her name, and then Becky wiped her eyes and hobbled away.

Our friends and neighbors began to file into the church.

I looked over my shoulder at them as Uncle Gus led us along the brick sidewalk to his Belair. We were going home until it was time for the actual service.

At the Belair my grandfather embraced my mother in his stunted, Old-Yankee way, and then my grandmother put her arms around her and cried on her shoulder, something that knocked my mother's hat loose and made her stiffen.

They walked on to their own car. Julie, Alvin and I got in the back of Uncle Gus's, and he held the door for our mother. Behind the wheel he lit a cigarette and blew smoke out the window. He shifted and drove us down the hill toward the bridge. We rode down the River Road, past his own house, and a mile farther past the still torn-up roadside where our father had crashed. Then Uncle Gus took a last drag on the cigarette and dropped it sparking onto the road.

We turned up our driveway and stopped behind my grandparents' pickup. Uncle Gus swung around in the front seat, red-faced, trying to think of something to say. Finally he just said, "We'll have to give it some time."

My mother got out and tugged sharply at her dress. She walked toward the house without waiting for us, moving stiffly, as if she were still marching in a parade.

Inside my grandparents slumped at the kitchen table, ignoring cups of coffee. My mother and Uncle Gus poured some for themselves and sat down, too. I went upstairs and flopped on my bunk and looked blankly out the window at the field and the woods.

My mind was busy and I was trying to ignore the dark shapes and dismal echoes: shadowy stuff that came home with me from the service. I wasn't managing very well. There was a lot of swirling and clashing going on in there, and trying to keep it under control made my head feel hot and loose.

Alvin came in and climbed the ladder into the upper bunk, which was set at right angles to mine. (Our father had built them that way to fit into a corner, one bunk against each wall, the head of Alvin's over the foot of mine, with space for a little coat closet under his.)

"Alvin?" I said,

He shifted his weight, making his bunk creak.

"I really hate this."

He still didn't answer.

"Don't you hate it?"

"Shut up, Cal."

I turned on my side and looked out the window.

Julie walked by on the landing and I heard her bedroom door open and shut. I looked at the blond-wood side of Alvin's bunk and thought of our father in that dark coffin. There were angry flashes in my head and I remembered the fire in my mother's eyes and thought I must be feeling what she was feeling. They were going to close that coffin up tight and bury him in the ground. I couldn't bear the thought. My eyes flooded and I felt tightness in my chest.

After a while our mother came upstairs, her footsteps slow and tired, and said, "Let's go," and we all dragged ourselves out of our rooms and followed her back down.

It was warm in the packed church. A housefly buzzed against the stained-glass window opposite our pew and people were murmuring. Father Daly came out in his white priest garb with the purple stole, palms pressed together in front of his chin. He stepped up to the lectern and the murmuring stopped.

Father Daly cleared his throat. "Let us p-p-pray." He held his hands out and began to chant. He didn't stutter when he chanted, his voice just rolled on and on, and I stopped listening and just let the buzz of his words sit in my mind.

When he finished we all made the sign of the cross. Father Daly stuttered through a eulogy, highlighting high points in John Shaw's life: his Eagle Scout success, his exploits on the baseball field, his stint as a petty officer during the war, his service as a town father.

Then he offered us a sampling of scripture.

I felt the reality of it like a rain cloud. Then this was shot through with a dull, sooty anger. I couldn't let it show, and that made me claustrophobic, and it didn't help that Uncle Gus was rocking minutely forward and back, as if he couldn't get comfortable.

Alvin took his glasses off and pinched his eyes shut. I was sure he was trying not to cry. On the other side of him, Julie's mouth hung open and trembled, and her shiny eyes were fixed on Father Daly. She made a choking sound and my mother looked at her for a moment and put an arm around her, but it looked even more awkward than usual, and Julie didn't seem to find much comfort there.

Father Daly said a final prayer and asked if anyone had memories to share, and a few men walked self-consciously up to the lectern to tell stories about hunting trips and golf matches and state championship games. When they were done, Father Daly stood from his chair against the wall and took a step toward reclaiming the lectern. But Uncle Gus surprised him by rising to say, "Excuse me." Father Daly looked at him, and Uncle Gus sidestepped out of our pew.

Father Daly backed up and sat down.

Uncle Gus took the lectern, tugged at his jacket, cleared his throat, and started talking. He had a hard time looking at anyone, and his voice was tight and squeaky, but he didn't give up. He told us how he'd gotten to know John Shaw because they'd had the same last name and the navy did everything alphabetically. This—along with a shared love of music (Gus an accomplished musician, my father a slappy, self-taught piano player)—made it easy to be friends, and when they shipped out together, they got even closer.

Uncle Gus had been a Midwest foster child, and had no real family, so after the war he'd followed John Shaw back to Maine, where he'd found an old ranch house to fix up on the same stretch of road where his best friend settled with his new wife (a pretty volunteer nurse's aide they'd met on shore leave in San Francisco, and of whom Jack had said, after two dates, "I do believe that might be the girl I'm going to marry!").

Uncle Gus had more to say. I don't remember the phrasing, but he was basically confessing just how much his own happiness had depended on John Shaw. (Which we already knew: He'd stayed a bachelor, and we'd been his family; his good times were hunting or fishing or music at our house, or anything else, really, that involved spending time with my father.) Finally his voice cracked and he gripped the lectern—shoulders up and large head low—until he'd regained control, and then his hands fell to his sides and he said, "We're just going to miss him, that's all. There's really no way around it. We're all going to miss Jack Shaw like hell."

Which made pious Father Daly frown.

But it made Julie catch her breath, and seemed to me to be exactly the truth of the thing.

SIX

Tampa, 1995

Despite Neal the Nazi's driving habits, we make it to the office of the taxi service—a shack a mile down the access road from the airport—and I sign out my cab and hang the clipboard back on its hook on the wall, to the left of the manager's desk.

Emile Lopez is the manager. He's skinny as a fence post, so everybody calls him Fats, or sometimes, El Gordo. Today he's wearing an un-tucked Hawaiian shirt that hangs loosely on him.

"Watch the oil, all right, Shaw?" he says.

I look at his skeptical face, with its horsey upper lip.

"I don't want to put another goddamn engine in that thing."

"I'll keep an eye on it."

He waves at me and goes back to his paperwork.

I walk out to the lot and fire up the old blue Chevy I've been saddled with since I got out of jail. (Fats let another driver commandeer the Crown Victoria I'd been driving, reasonably enough, since they had no way to know when I'd be back.)

It takes a few seconds to warm up, then I drive out of the lot and down the access road and around to the taxi stand by baggage claim.

Delta has just come in from New York, and I grab a couple of pleasant old-timers heading into Clearwater to see what shape their winter renters left the condo. They're on the spring-training rental list, and some of the minor leaguers can be rambunctious. But my passengers love the idea of being associated with professional baseball, so they don't really mind.

Traffic is still crawling because of the potato truck, but these people are too nice to be impatient, and as we make our way toward the causeway, they tell me what various young ballplayers have done to their property. Then they get into the past winter and how much snow they had and how long the dirty snowbanks lasted.

Here in Florida it's sweltering, and my AC isn't much, but my new *no importa* attitude is holding up all right. I don't mind the heat or the small talk. And after a while, when the conversation runs down, I get my passengers' permission to put the radio on. The local jazz station in St. Pete is featuring Miles Davis today; his muted trumpet seems just right.

It's pretty on the causeway, with the little fishing boats circling in the bay and the sunlight on the water and the bait fishermen casting from the pedestrian shoulder.

Miles is playing "Blue in Green," and as I watch gulls gliding overhead and sunlight on the water and girls walking the bridge in pairs, with their hair shifting in the breeze, I suddenly feel that earlier mood again. I'm grateful to be here at this moment, seeing what I'm seeing and hearing Miles—and Coltrane and Chambers and Bill Evans—calling and answering about their personal knowledge of the sad beauty of life.

Then we thump off the causeway and I have to dodge a panel truck taking a quick, risky slant across my lane, and just like that I'm back in business mode.

I drop my passengers and head back across the causeway. Traffic is starting to improve, and by the time Fats has bounced me around Tampa for a couple of hours, it is no more sluggish than usual.

Then it becomes just another day. I'm hustling the same as always, working the side streets to make time, playing my passengers for tips, and I don't have time for nostalgia or deep thinking. (I do carry in the back of my mind a thought about making a trip across the Skyway Bridge, because I want to look down at the water and see how it feels up there on that high span. But I never get far enough south.)

The sun moves across the sky and it gets even warmer and I make trips with airmen to McGill, a long run to Winter Haven, and do lots of running around town. And maybe it's my new attitude, but by the time my shift ends and I've headed for the barn to turn the old Chevy back in, I've had my best money day in a long time.

It makes me smile, the way things work sometimes.

At the office, Fats is grumpy when he hands me a note scribbled in smudged pencil. He doesn't like taking messages and won't make any effort to jot them down legibly. But I manage to work out that it's from a friend named Henderson who runs a little jazz club on North Franklin.

I wonder if it was he who called me at home that morning, but when I borrow Fats's phone and call he claims it wasn't. He'd only that afternoon heard from Tampa Red that their horn player had had to sneak out of town for domestic reasons, and they needed a stand-in for two nights.

"You sure it wasn't you?"

"Use your head, Cal. What the hell would I be doing up before dawn?"

"Good point."

"So are you in? Else I'm going to have to call around."

"That's not much notice."

"You can handle it."

I wonder for a moment if my blazer is clean enough for a gig—
Red's combos always sport blue blazers—and then I say, "All right,
what the hell."

"Good." I hear someone talking in the background, and then
he comes back on. "Red's asking do you want to get together and go
over the list?"

"Nah, I'm fine." I've heard Red's band before, most recently at an
Al Downing event just before I was locked up. They play the usual
West Coast stuff: the Chet Baker, Miles and Gerry Mulligan cool jazz,
which is right up my alley.

"And you've got it all under control?" Hendu says.

"Oh, yeah."

"You wouldn't bullshit me."

"I got squared away at Pinellas."

"That must have been fun."

"Yeah, not so much."

I remember lying on my bunk in the kick tank, shaking and
nauseous.

"Okay, then. Eight o'clock."

I hang up the phone just as Fats is about to give me hell for tying
up one of his business lines. He eyes me anyway as I walk over to the
cabbie card table, drop my cash bag, pull out my receipts and fare sheets
and start figuring my forty percent of the take with the old calculator.

"You make me any money?"

"Millions," I say.

There's a roar as a jet takes off. It flies close overhead, rattling the
windows. Fats's office is off the end of a short runway that's only used
when the wind is right.

"So how much did you steal?"

"No more than was reasonable."

He snorts a laugh.

I give him the paperwork and his share of the cash, then ask him to sport me a ride back to Dearborne Street. He rolls his eyes and wonders when I'm going to break down and buy a frigging mo-ped or something, but then presses the transmitter key. "All stations alert! We got a deadbeat here needs a ride."

"A mo-ped?" I say.

"A scooter, then. Whatever. A fucking mule."

The radio crackles. "Let me guess, that *pendejo* Shaw."

"*Si*," Fats says. "He says you can charge him double. It's all the same to him."

Fats laughs. His jokes are almost always for his own benefit.

"Five minutes," the voice says, and clicks off.

"Thanks a lot, Fats."

He grunts.

"I appreciate it."

Fats squints up at me. "You're awful goddamn sweet today."

I make prayer hands and bow my head. Fats waves me off and I go outside to wait. It's still warm, and I lean on the chain-link fence and fight off wanting a drink. (*Just one!* my friendly little demon whispers. *Just a beer! It's so hot out!*)

I kick at the dusty spikes of grass growing through the bottom of the fence and watch another passenger jet taking off on the short runway. The jet barrels along, wings sagging, gathering speed. Then its nose jerks up as if it is leaving the ground at a sharp angle, but really it's just plowing slightly upward and forward, in a chesty sort of way, when it thunders over the shack.

The roar fades and I hear a beep and turn to see my old Crown Vic—number seven—coming up. It stops opposite where I stand and the driver gives me a wise-guy smile. He has thick, black hair slicked back and a pencil-thin mustache and wears a black sleeveless T-shirt that shows off the ropy muscles in his arms.

I get in and he puts his hand on the meter as if to throw it. When I just smile, he says, "Bah!", and pulls himself back behind the wheel. "How's that Chev-ro-lay working for you?" he says, looking over his shoulder at the road.

"It's a peach."

He grins.

"Go ahead with the meter."

"That's all right, *chico*. I'll take you in out of the goodness of my heart."

He throws the gearshift and drives toward the road.

"You're a good man."

"I'm a fool," he says. "But I can't help it."

There's a gap in the oncoming traffic and he steps on it to merge. We snake out into the traffic and head north. He has his radio on, and is flicking cigarette ash out the window, and we listen to cha-cha music all the way in.

When he lets me off at the trailer park I stick a sawbuck in his ashtray and jump out before he can refuse it. Then I grin like I've put one over on him.

He drives off, tapping the horn lightly.

I look at the kids' trailer, but it feels empty.

Inside my own I ignore another sharp craving for cold beer—there's none in the place anyway; I'd have to go out—and settle for a glass of water.

I sit down on my bed and dig a blank music sheet out of my old portfolio, so I can set down the melody that's back in my head again.

I take out the Olds, play a couple of bars, and score it. Then I play a little more, muting so that no one will come thumping on my door because their afternoon siesta has been interrupted.

I cross a section out on the sheet and rewrite it. Then I put the sheet away and just blow for an hour, warming up for Henderson's. I play scales and a few easy pieces and work my way into "Blue in Green," trying to make it sound like Miles, and then I mess around in different voices: Clark Terry, Chet, Lee Morgan, Dizzy. (I was always pretty good at imitation; it's an important part of how I learned to play back in those days when the trumpet was all I had, after it seemed like I'd lost everything else.)

Afterwards I go back to my new melody and fiddle with that until I have to stop, because without meaning to, I've conjured up something very weepy and raw, something that has to do with Julie, or maybe her ghost. (I know I haven't told you much about Julie yet; I just haven't found the right moment to be direct about it. But trust me, I'm working up to it.)

I hold the cornet in my lap as the old emotions rise; for the sake of the music I let them knock around inside, dark and lumpy and mean as can be.

Bent over the horn with my elbows on my knees, I feel all the old cruel scenes play themselves out; I hold them in my mind until my stomach twists and I remember about the barn and what happened there and how unfair it all was.

I hold my breath against another fierce desire to drink, then exhale and tell my sweet sister that maybe pretty soon we'll be together again, and we'll be able to talk as much as she wants. But that doesn't help;

she wants to talk now. And I can't stop her. It's like another melody has come along that has to be heard—only I know where this one goes, and there's nothing I have to do but let it play.

I see the two of us in the hayloft, Julie tossing her head and stepping out onto the timbers that run all the way across to the wall above the double doors. I watch her walk across and then start back and I face up to the swirling dark colors that form into tumbling shapes and I hold on tight.

This is a bad one, but I've outlasted bad ones before, and eventually it all starts to smooth out. Then everything settles a little more, and it's not much longer until I can let go.

I hang my head, spot a soiled T-shirt in a heap of laundry on the floor, and grab it to blow my nose. I drop the T-shirt, raise the horn, and press it to my lips for a moment, and then I play my melody through again, trying to let it just speak.

I'm talking back to Julie now, the best way I can.

I follow the shape of our conversation, turning and expanding along one edge, and I work it out that way until everything matches, and I see the shape shift again, and I play along the new path for a few more bars, and then I start from the beginning and play it all again, hearing the piano chords in my head, and I jot it down on the music sheet, writing around a couple of damp spots on the paper.

SEVEN

Tampa, 1995

Tampa Red is in good form, but he has a new drummer who manages to consistently come down exactly in the middle of the beat. You or I couldn't manage it if we tried, but he does it naturally, and nothing anyone else plays seems to make any difference. That's bad, because it can make it hard to really swing, which is the main idea, right?

But I'm able to work with it, which is encouraging. I haven't played in public for some time, and haven't played *straight* in public for years. I could never neglect my horn for long—even fall-down drunk I was likely to haul it out and start blowing—but performing for an audience, with other musicians, is a whole different ball of wax.

But I'm doing all right. The ideas are there, and once I get warmed up, I find I'm still capable of chasing them into a decent shape. Not setting the world on fire, maybe, but no liability, either. And it gets better as we go along.

When we're soloing and it drops to me, I know where to go and how to do it. I know how to pick up Red's lines and throw them back at him; how to build off his digression and make it into my own; how to bring it all back to where we started. It feels really, really good, and even better when our audience applauds and whistles and Red looks at me and nods.

There's a good crowd, and it's smoky and dark in the little joint. My old amigo Rocky Kincaid is there; he looked me up after he got out of the pokey, and then figured Tampa was as good a place as any to hang his hat. (He's from Mississippi, but nomadic, and was just passing through when he ran afoul of the law, as they say.)

Kincaid is sitting at one of the old two-tops near the windows with a tall, lovely gal—no surprise, with Kincaid—who hasn't been shy about clapping and even whistling when she likes something we've done. When we take a break I step down from the little foot-high stage and go over to say hello. Rocky kicks a chair out so I can sit down. I take the blazer off and drape it over the back of the chair.

"This is Celeste Boucher," Rocky says. He's grinning and his forehead is shiny. "She's a trumpet girl, and she's got a big crush on you. She says you look like Quaid, man! Quaid with a trumpet! Now how am I supposed to compete with that?"

"I'm sure you're worried about it."

Celeste shakes my hand and smiles.

"I was telling her about our tats, man." Rocky rolls up the sleeve of his pink dress shirt, exposing the tattoo he got in jail: a little blue sax with a flurry of sixteenth notes flying out of its bell.

"She's never seen that?"

"Oh hell, yeah, she's seen mine." He pokes at my sleeve, and I roll it up past my own tattoo, which is like Rocky's, only with a trumpet. Celeste reaches over and touches the tattoo on my inner forearm. It gives me a tingle and she smiles as if she knew it would.

"Tell her the story," Rocky says. "You tell it better than me."

"She doesn't want to hear all that."

"It's a good story!"

"Good and boring." I smile at Celeste.

"Nah, man, it's a tragic tale of . . . something."

"Of nothing."

"No, it's definitely of something. Me and you, brother. Two jazzmen locked up in the can. Remember when we played for the warden?"

He winks at Celeste.

"We never played for the warden."

"We did when I tell it. Remember how he offered to commute us?"

"Wardens can't commute sentences."

"Celeste don't know that. She's from the swamp country."

"Oh, Rocky," Celeste smiles tolerantly.

"All right," Rocky says, "she probably knows. So forget that. What did the warden do? He let us bunk together, and instead of peeling potatoes, we got to wail for the population."

Which was true: The warden liked jazz, and offered to let us skip work detail and practice if we'd perform for the inmates. So we did, and a guy who played piano joined us, and then we got a drummer (who was better than Tampa Red's drummer, by the way), and just like that, we had a combo.

We weren't that bad. Kincaid could play, and the keyboard dude had some chops, and I'd been out of the kick tank long enough to stop shaking. One day the four of us decided to get the tattoos from a con who had a little business going. Thinking about it, I wonder what's happened to the other two guys.

Rocky's still inventing jail-time adventures for Celeste—making us both laugh—when I hear piano chords from the little staging area. I look over and Red is sitting at the piano, looking back with his eyebrows up.

I roll my sleeve back down. "Time to go to work."

"Break a leg!" Rocky says, and Celeste says, "Nice to meet you," and when I get back to the stand I see that she's watching with her hands clasped under her chin.

It's been a good crowd all night. Most of the other people have been paying attention too, and Henderson himself, standing behind the bar in his green apron—*The color of money, brother*—has had a smile on his face most of the night.

I pick up my horn and just like that, Red launches the intro to "Joy Spring," and I have ten seconds to get myself ready to go. I give him a look, but I'm there and he laughs, and then we're at the break and I do my best Brownie imitation.

The whole set is fast—Red likes to work that way—and we play "Daahoud" and a couple more quick ones, and then we're cooking along in the middle of a Thelonious number called "Well, You Needn't," playing it fast, like on *Chet Is Back!* Red is comping sweet, two-handed chords while I chase after a flexy shape that snakes through the chords, nasty and abrupt, like a used pipe cleaner.

I've maintained my fluency as the night's gone on, and now something clicks and I nip up as close as I ever get to master territory, nailing a phrase so precisely—when it really shouldn't have fit—that I hear Celeste Boucher laugh out loud and somebody else whistles.

That's a good feeling; maybe the best.

So I have some drive when the pay phone on the wall starts in, and I'm able to keep on for a while, playing through the shrillness, but the damn thing won't stop, and finally I give Red a look, take a shortcut back to the melody and let it go.

I lower my horn, and while our bass man twongs his way up through my applause, I see Henderson come out of the back room, lean across the bar, and snatch the phone off its cradle.

He listens, then holds it against his chest and jerks his head for me to come over. I tuck the Olds under my arm, suspicious as to whether it might be the same person who called that morning.

Heads turn to see where I'm going.

Henderson holds out the receiver, then walks back to the triple beer taps to wait on a new customer. I duck my head close to the wall.

"Make it quick."

I hear: "Cal?"

And man, that's all it takes. I mean, my mind has been halfway there for days anyway. I press my forehead against the wall and shut my eyes. I see flickers of the house, the family, the old, paint-peeled barn. I see my father and my mother, and I see that piece of shit Pike (his meat-eater grin, grizzly-bear shoulders and black mustache), and then I see Julie in the hayloft, defiant and brave.

"Cal!" Alvin says again.

I look at the stage, where Red is hunched over the keyboard, shaking his head and playing like there's no tomorrow.

"Say something, man!"

"Hey," I say, finally. "Okay. Alvin."

"Jesus, it's about time."

"I'm sorry." I cover my off-ear with a hand so I can hear him better.

"You're not an easy guy to talk to, little brother."

"Was that you this morning?"

"I've been trying all day. Finally had to track down your probation officer."

I picture the PO, a little man named Swanson who is probably fifty years old and still wears his hair in bangs. I remember he had potted plants in front of his window that he puttered with while we talked, poking his finger in the dirt, snapping off bits. He insisted on family information, so he could copy them in. I didn't know if that was required, or just something he thought would help, but at that point I only wanted to get the hell out, and would have signed off on anything.

Alvin got my work number from Swanson, and then Fats told him about the message from Henderson, and since the club was called Henderson's, the rest of it was doable enough.

"You went to a lot of trouble," I say.

"Well, it was important."

Which is when I realize that there has to be a reason for the call, and something that looks like a sunspot, black-rimmed and fiery, goes off in my head.

"Wait," I say. "Not the old lady?"

"She's fine."

I peek over my shoulder at Red, sitting upright now, banging the keys, an ashy cigarette in his mouth. Who knows how he managed to fish it out of his pocket and light it without missing a beat.

"Don't tell me it's Pike."

"No, it's Uncle Gus."

"Oh, no."

Turns out he'd suffered a stroke—fell off his chair watching television and stayed on the floor until morning, when one of his music students spotted him through the window. Now he's in the hospital, unable to speak, but, according to Alvin, able to focus when you talk to him.

"Man," I say.

"Yeah. I thought you'd want to know." He waits, and when I don't say anything more, he says, "So do you think you might come back?"

"I probably should, huh?"

"You're the one he liked."

"He liked you, too."

"Yeah, but I didn't play the trumpet."

That's true, and I don't say anything.

"If you need money . . . "

"No, I'm good."

"All right, then."

He goes silent again, and I know he's waiting for me to confirm that I'll be heading home, which we both know I haven't quite done. And I would, if I hadn't suddenly lost the ability to speak.

Uncle Gus was the only ally I had after things really went sour. He even let me move in with him when I had to leave home. So even though he never actually defended me—he was too afraid of Pike—I still always had feelings for him.

"You still there?" Alvin says.

I clear my throat. "Yeah."

"So I wouldn't wait too long."

"Got it."

"Seriously."

"All right. Is he in Portland?"

"Yeah, Maine Medical. You could go right in from the airport. I could meet you there and bring you back. You'll have to stay at the old homestead, though; I don't have a lot of space left over, what with the kids . . . "

"Don't worry about that."

"Oh, I wasn't." He cackles, then goes silent, and after a minute or so I figure the conversation has pretty much run its course. But I want to end on a decent note, so I break into the silence to thank him for calling.

"No problem."

"I'm glad everybody else is okay."

"We're struggling along. How about you?"

"I'm doing all right."

"Are you playing much?"

"Well, I'm playing tonight."

I watch Red and his crew walk toward the bar, where Hendu is setting them up with beers. Red looks at me and shrugs as if to say *I couldn't wait forever.*

"Well, Alvin says, "I'll see you if I see you."

Then I'm listening to the dial tone. I shake my head. Fucking Alvin.

I hang the phone up, open the spit valve on my horn, shake a few drops out onto the floor next to the smudged mopboard.

Henderson comes down, leans on the short side of the bar, and looks at me.

"My uncle had a stroke." I give the cornet a last shake.

"I'm sorry, man. Were you close?"

"Pretty close."

"Is it serious?"

"Sounds like it might be."

He nods. "Go ahead and split, then."

"I can't do anything about it tonight."

"You go ahead. Get things together."

I fiddle with the valves, tempted to insist that I finish out the two nights. But then Henderson taps a finger on the bar and says, "You do what's right, Calvin."

I go back to the stage and lay the Olds onto its worn velvet, then snap the clasps and swing by the bar again to tell Red what's going on. It's gotten noisy with bar chatter since the music stopped, and he leans in close and says, "Get in touch when you get back."

I shake his hand, nod to the other two guys, and walk across the room to Kincaid's table.

"What's up, man?

"Got a call from home."

"*Home* home?"

"My uncle. I guess he had a stroke."

"The uncle that played?"

We'd talked a lot in jail.

"Yeah."

"Anything I can do?"

"No, but thanks."

Celeste Boucher reaches out a small, mocha-shaded hand. "I'm so sorry about your uncle."

"Thanks."

"I love your playing."

"Thank you."

She smiles sadly. Smart eyes, world-class dimples, thin-strapped print dress square across her chest. I pull my gaze away from her and shake hands with Kincaid.

"You need any cash?"

"I'm good."

"All right. You know where to find me."

I head out, winding through the tables, tapping the palms of a couple of guys along the way.

When I get to the door I see Henderson stalking the perimeter of the room, so I wait. He comes up and sticks a wad of bills into my hand.

"Almost forgot."

"You don't need to do that."

"Nah, man, you helped me out on short notice."

"Now I'm leaving you high and dry."

"Take the bread; just keep your head on straight. Don't fuck it up now that you've got this far, okay?" He nods and marches in his muscular way back to the bar.

I slip the cash into my blazer pocket and step out into the night.

Wispy steam rises from sewer grates, and cars cruise past with their headlights on, dragging thumping bass lines from souped-up stereos.

A young couple comes around the corner. The guy is air force, and his girl is dressed like a hippie, with a long skirt and a tight jersey. They go into the club and I think of my own crazy nights with various girls, and I feel a sudden, strong tug to step back into that life. It always looks less dangerous from a distance. You remember the carefree existence, you feel nostalgic for the parties and camaraderie and access to women that even a modestly successful jazzman can have (especially in New York), and you minimize the hazards.

All I want at that moment is to get buzzed and find some lady to try and drunk-charm. I know it's a false feeling, I do. But I still have to concentrate to keep it from taking me over like it's done in the past.

I run away from the club, crossing the intersection, dodging past a low-slung car that isn't about to slow down for the likes of me. I jump up on the curb, banging the case against my leg, and head for a shortcut between a used-clothing store and a boarded-up head shop. The clothing store has a nightlight on behind its plate-glass window, and I can see two well-dressed adult and a couple of kid mannequins, sitting around a picnic table, all smiling ferociously.

I trot down the alley and come out into a hardscrabble neighborhood of apartment buildings and beat-up old frame homes. There are some tough-guy adolescents on one corner, and they turn to look at me, but note the cornet case and only nod. I suppose they're used to musicians coming and going from Henderson's.

Once through that neighborhood, I make a left turn and stay in the shadows to skirt a liquor store with cars in its lot with their lights on. A few blocks later the buildings thin out and there are abandoned houses and weedy, littered, vacant lots with chain-link fences.

I keep going, and after another half-hour I'm on outer Dearborne. It's darker without all the city lights and I have four miles to go to reach my Home Sweet (Tin) Home.

EIGHT

Tampa, 1995

I hike along Dearborne and stick out my thumb, but no one shows the least interest in stopping. So after a while I just resign myself to walking the whole way.

It's no big deal. I'm not going to waste money paying for a taxi, nor impose on one of my fellow cabbies when they're hustling to finish off the night. It's warm anyway, and walking makes it easier to think.

I walk along the gravel shoulder, passing rural homes with scruffy yards and ramshackle garages, some advertising small businesses (a vacuum cleaner repair shop; an outfit called Snowbird Auto Sales).

It's well after midnight now, and the good feeling from playing again has faded and I'm stuck in that loneliness that can crop up when you're out by yourself in the wee hours.

I look up at the stars—bright pinpricks—and I think about how that light came from far in the past, and my mind sort of lurches sideways to my own past, and home, and I try to imagine going back after all this time.

It's such an unexpected possibility. It's been twenty-odd years, which until tonight would have seemed like a long time, but which now, suddenly, feels like hardly any time at all.

My thoughts go back to the old farmhouse on the river, and it's good, at first. It was my world, after all, and I knew every corner of that building and every inch of the property. My family was everything, and for ten years there I felt invincible.

But it doesn't take long to lose that good feeling.

The bad stuff—my father, my sister and Pike—comes crowding into the picture as usual. It boils and intensifies, and before long I have to stop, turn my cornet case on end, and sit down for a time-out. Sometimes you just have to have a cigarette and trust that those dark, squirmy thoughts will back off.

So I sit there, next to a spiky telephone pole.

It's quiet, with the occasional car that you can hear coming from a long way off. The air is still and thick. My shirt is stuck to my back and now the mosquitoes have found me.

I blow smoke at them and take another drag and my mind begins to settle, and when I can think clearly again I consider the two halves of my childhood, how they split starting with my father's death and then broke wide open after Julie's. It was as if my father's accident opened a malevolent door to all the other bad stuff; I think that if he'd only stayed alive, none of it would have happened.

But he didn't stay alive, and I remember how my life was yanked off its rails that summer with him gone, and I remember, too, how awfully different things were when I went back to school in the fall.

It was like being a new kid almost, since I was the only one in my class who had ever lost a parent. Other kids looked at me sideways and the teachers walked on eggshells, trying not to say the wrong thing. And I had my role to play, too. I could no longer be one of the rambunctious kids. I was already sad, and this made me angry, which only added to my problems.

There wasn't much help at home, either.

My father had been our family's center of gravity, and now that he was gone, everything was stretched loose and my mother just wasn't capable of taking up the slack.

That wasn't all her fault, I grant you. She'd been brought up without any love, right? (Or maybe worse; I never found out for sure.) Then she'd finally found some with Jack Shaw, and now he'd stupidly taken that away, and she was really angry and lost (just like I was).

It must have been overwhelming to try and deal with that and take care of three kids. She also had to go out and find a job, when she'd never had to work. So probably I should consider all that and excuse her to a certain extent.

But more than twenty years later—sitting on my cornet case, slapping bugs, squinting into the past—it's still hard to go all the way with that. I'm still angry that she didn't find some better way to cope. People do fight through their limitations when they have to rise to the occasion, do they not?

I mean, there were kids involved.

I do believe her own cold-fish parents left her with a small, stony heart, and that my father had found the one piece of it still capable of love, and that when he deserted her by drinking and driving and dying, that little soft spot was torn apart and had to calcify to heal at all. And I also believe that when that healing took place, it didn't leave much room for me or my brother and sister.

But I'm still not excusing her. Because even if that soft spot was gone, she should have known enough to pretend. She could have faked it, and we wouldn't have known the difference. We were only kids, right?

We were only kids.

BIG MAN

NINE

Baxter, Fall, 1964

She had no choice anymore but to get after it.

We would come home from school and she'd be at the kitchen table with the classifieds, circling anything that looked promising.

She'd have an ashtray there with stubbed-out cigarettes, and a cup of cold coffee with an oily-looking slick. When we came in she'd look up and say, "Hello, children. Have your snack and go watch TV, please." There'd be a box of graham crackers waiting for us on the table, and a jar of Skippy peanut butter, the crunchy kind. Then she'd go back to the newspaper while we got glasses of milk and sat down with her to have our snack.

"Anything good?" one of us might say.

Without looking up she'd say, "We'll see."

That's how it went that first week. She pored over the classifieds, made phone calls while we watched our shows, and sometimes put on the gray Chanel skirt and jacket she'd bought because of Jackie Kennedy and drive off for an interview.

There seemed to be plenty of jobs in the newspaper—we were still in the postwar boom—and it only took a week for her to settle on becoming a nurse's aide at the Pen Bay Medical Center. She went in to apply and was hired on the spot.

The following Monday morning, she told us that Julie would be in charge at home—which made Alvin and me scowl—until she got home from work. She taped Uncle Gus's number on the wall by the phone in case of an emergency, then sent us out to wait for the bus.

It was drizzling, so we waited in the old vegetable stand. I remember the rain pattering on the roof as we looked out at the wet road. When the bus stopped we waited until Mabel Morrison opened the door and ran for it.

We were almost to the bridge when our mother swooshed past, water spraying up from her tires, on her way to the hospital. She was going pretty fast, and my hopes raced right along with her.

But that job only lasted a month.

Her Red Cross training didn't stand up to the reality of blood, bedpans, and urine-soaked johnnies. The leaky fluids of strangers made her ill, and she couldn't offset this through gallows humor or camaraderie like the other CNAs, because she didn't know how, and because her husband had died. So she gave notice, and went back to the classifieds.

Her second attempt was as an assistant to old Doc Weatherbee, the dentist, who sported the only goatee in the village. But that one didn't last much longer than the hospital job. It just wasn't a good fit. My mother was even less sociable than she'd been before, and Dr. Weatherbee's patients soon decided she was snooty. Everybody knew she'd grown up in godless California, which made that no real surprise. And they understood that her husband had died, but they were a war generation that had lost lots of husbands, and they thought she needed to move on like everyone else.

So Dr. Weatherbee fired her and replaced her with an older woman who may not have dressed up the office like my mother but was much better with the patients.

I don't recall what the third job was, but she failed again, and by that time nearly three months had passed with only a few small paychecks to show for it. So things had gotten very tight, and she was getting desperate when she spotted the new help-wanted ad placed by the Randall Pike Real Estate Agency.

Everybody knew old pig-eyed Randy Pike, who was something of a local legend. He'd gotten his real estate license while still in high school, had started his own business two years after graduating, and had been smart—or lucky—enough to buy up farmland along the upper river just before the big development push in Knox County.

That made him a shitload of money, and also elevated him to Big Man status in our little town. Even a messy divorce—with rumors about an underage babysitter—couldn't touch him. And after he broke Arthur Stimpson's nose at the Neutral Corner bar for making a crack about jailbait, everybody decided to leave the topic alone.

So my mother knew exactly who she'd be dealing with, but it didn't matter, she was desperate. And it didn't matter that Pike was looking for a licensed agent, either; she was sure they could find a way to work around that.

She put on the Chanel outfit, drove straight to his office, and in a twenty-minute interview managed to convince him that it made perfect sense to let her start as a sort of receptionist until she could pass the real estate test and truly join the team.

At supper that night she said, "Let's hope this pans out," and explained that if it did and she sold lots of homes, maybe when the time was right she could go into business for herself. Then they wouldn't have to depend on anybody. "So keep your fingers crossed," she said, and it seemed to me at the time that some light had come back into her eyes.

I crossed my fingers behind my back, and I suspect Alvin and Julie did, too. And just in case it helped, that night I prayed hard on my knees for this one to work out. I prayed so hard that when Julie came up the stairs and passed my open door I didn't even try to disguise what I was doing. I stayed on my knees and prayed that this job would be one my mother could keep and that would be the first step back for our family—or if not exactly back, at least away from what we'd become, which was basically just a collection of unhappy people.

For a little while it seemed that my prayers might be answered. My mother studied hard and passed the written test on her first try. She went to the hairdresser's for a short, modern trim and bought some more business-y clothes. And at first, with Pike feeding her clients and helping show the properties, she didn't do badly. But eventually she had to go out on her own and then it all went to hell. It turned out she was no better at real estate than she'd been at dirty bedpans or crusty molars: her chilly personality again.

She never made even one sale by herself, and that put Pike in a bind. He was businessman enough to know he had to take her off the roster; she was losing business, and his other agents were starting to grumble.

But there was a complication: He and my mother had already become something of a couple. Maybe this was my mother cold-bloodedly hedging her bets, but however it happened, despite their difference in age (he was eight years younger), they'd become cozy enough that Pike was taking her out on Saturday nights, and doing chores for her, like plowing our driveway after it snowed.

That wasn't the only plowing he had in mind, but my mother managed to keep him somewhat in check, which wasn't easy with a man who had trouble taking no for an answer. I saw this myself one evening when he'd come over after supper and I'd slipped out the side door to spy on them and caught them smooching on the porch, leaning together from separate rocking chairs.

Peering through the slats at the end of the porch railing, I saw him snort and paw, and my mother suddenly stand, tug at her clothes, and tell him she was sorry, but she wasn't ready for that sort of thing, yet. After which he grabbed her by the shoulders. "You seem pretty ready to me," he said, and pulled her close against him. She struggled and said, "No, Randy!" but he just held her tighter and tried to kiss her.

Before I could climb over the railing one of the rockers went over with a bang, and that seemed to snap him out of the state he'd been in.

He laughed and held up his palms. "Sorry, kid, I guess I got carried away."

"I'll say good night." My mother turned and opened the door.

When the door closed behind her Pike stared at it for a moment, then turned and smashed the heel of his hand against a porch post hard enough that I thought it might crack. It made me jump, but he didn't hear me.

He marched down the steps and walked to his pickup, kicking a leg out to adjust himself along the way. I knew that had to do with men and women, and what he'd wanted to do with my mother, and I wished I'd had a rock that I could wing at his head.

Afterwards my mother didn't tell him to get lost, and they kept right on as if nothing had happened, and that's how things stood when Pike figured out what he had to do in terms of the workplace.

He liked to tell the story afterward—how he approached her at her desk and asked to talk to her in his office. How once inside the office, he shut the door and said, very seriously, "Have a seat, Betty."

I can see her sitting there, back straight, holding her pocketbook in her lap, no doubt in despair that she'd failed again.

"Are you going to fire me?" she said.

"Not exactly." Pike leaned against his desk with his arms crossed. Then he told her that she shouldn't worry; it didn't matter that selling real estate apparently wasn't her cup of tea, because he had another position for her to consider.

My mother cocked her head. "What's that, Randy?"

Pike grinned and reached back to open his desk drawer. He fished something out, then pushed away from the desk, sank heavily to one knee and presented the pretty little box in both hands.

TEN

Baxter, Late Winter, 1965

My mother told Pike that she'd need time to think, but I doubt he was very worried. He was Randy Pike, wasn't he? Besides, he knew that she didn't have a lot of options. She'd failed at working for a living, which meant that she pretty much had to marry someone or go bankrupt.

And it wasn't much of a seller's market either, not even for a looker like Betty Shaw; not if she was also pushing forty, with three kids and a mortgage. So I doubt he was shocked when she accepted a week later.

We were, though, when we found out about it the next morning.

As I remember, it was almost time to head outside for the bus. It wasn't spring yet, and still dark enough at that time of day that the light over the sink was on. We were slurping down our Cheerios (me) and Rice Krispies (Alvin and Julie) when our mother came over to the table and sat down.

We watched her, spoons hovering.

"I have something to tell you," she said, clearing her throat and looking seriously from one of us to the other. "And that is that Mr. Pike and I have decided to join forces."

"What does 'join forces' mean?"

My mother looked at Julie. "It means that we're going to get married." She was a little flushed around the cheekbones. "A few days ago Mr. Pike said he thought it was about time that we took the plunge. I told him I'd think about it, and last night I called him and said that the answer was yes."

I was too aghast at the idea to speak.

But Julie narrowed her eyes and said, "Shouldn't you have asked us first?"

"No. It was a decision I had to make."

"What if we don't want a new father?"

I thought I knew exactly how Julie felt: Pike dropping by or clearing the driveway or dating our mother was one thing. But Pike becoming part of our family was too horrible to even contemplate.

My mother quickly held up her hands. "Mr. Pike won't be trying to replace your father. He'll be your stepfather, is all. Now listen, I've invited him over for supper tonight—"

"Oh, joy."

"That's enough, Julia. He's coming over and we'll all get to know each other a little better." She looked at the clock over the stove. "Now finish up or you'll miss the bus." She stood, cinched her robe tighter, gave us a last look, and walked stiffly away.

We heard her going up the stairs.

"Holy crap," Alvin said.

Julie just scraped her chair back and took her bowl to the sink. Then she went to the coat closet in the hallway, banging the door open, looking furious.

Alvin and I finished our cereal and hurried to catch up.

We threw on our jackets, grabbed our lunch boxes and ran out the door and across the porch. We trotted down the driveway, past the barn.

The sun was coming up over the trees, but it was still cold. We'd had a false spring—in like a lamb—but then winter had come back crackling cold with sheets of ice forming along the banks of the river.

Our breath billowed as we walked down to the River Road. We piled our gear by the mailbox and stuffed our hands into our pockets and stomped our feet to stay warm. All the while we looked at each other as if to say *I can't believe it!*

Then Alvin said, "You know, we've actually got nobody to blame but ourselves." He said this in the *I'm-the-grown-up* voice Julie and I both hated, but I knew he had a point.

"How so?" Standing there in the cold, strands of blonde hair trailing out from under her knitted cap, still stiff with anger, Julie looked as pretty as our mother.

"We shouldn't have been so nice to him." Alvin kicked at the foot of the new snowbank.

"You and Cal, you mean."

"You were just as bad."

"Like heck I was!"

Alvin was right, though: We were all guilty. None of us had liked Pike from the start, but we'd pretended to because he was our mother's new boss and she needed all the help she could get. So we said "Hello, Mr. Pike!" when he came around, and when he said "Hello, you termites" back, Alvin and I would fake laughter, and even Julie would pretend to smile. And we never let on that we saw through him; that we'd caught him hiding his real, mean face behind phony smiles.

The bus came rattling down the road then.

We grabbed our stuff as it came to a stop in front of our driveway. Mabel Morrison—the only bus driver we'd ever known—cranked the door open and said, "Here's the Shaw tribe!" in the cheery voice she'd used since our father's accident.

We weren't in any mood to respond, and trudged past her single file down the gritty aisle. Alvin and I took one of the hard-springy seats—

no matter how we were getting along, we always sat together—and Julie joined Becky O'Dell, who lived downriver and always boarded before us.

I heard Julie whispering her outrage, but Alvin and I didn't speak.

Mabel ground the bus's gears and we hugged ourselves against the chill and looked out the window at the icy river as we jostled up the road toward town.

ELEVEN

Baxter, Late Winter, 1965

I shoved Billy White at recess that day and when he fell he scraped his knee and burst into tears. The principal used it as an excuse to sit me down with the guidance counselor again—lanky Mrs. Coffin—and she kept me occupied the rest of the afternoon, answering questions about my family and how we were coping with my father's "absence," or sitting silently at her desk while I declined to answer a particular question, or listening to tapes other guidance counselors had made about handling grieving children.

So I didn't get another chance to talk to Alvin about Pike until we were in line for the bus.

"Okay," he said then, "what can we do?"

We decided on the ride home that first of all, we should stop pretending we liked Pike, so our mother would notice and maybe reconsider. ("It's a woman's prerogative to change her mind" was one of her favorite sayings.)

As soon as we got off the bus we told Julie what we'd decided, and it turned out she'd already come to the same conclusion after talking it over with Becky O'Dell.

We pinkie-shook on it on the porch before going inside, where our mother—unemployed again—was busy peeling potatoes—*snick, snick*—into the sink.

"Hello, children," she said. "Your snack's on the table."

She was probably too preoccupied to notice any signs of insurrection that might have shown on our faces, but we ate fast anyway and got the hell out of there.

We were watching TV when we heard Pike in the kitchen.

"No chickening out," Julie said, and when Pike came into the living room and said, "Hello, you termites!" he was met with an uneasy silence, instead of the usual phony greetings. It was scary to do this, and I held my breath as the silence thickened in the room.

"What's the matter?" Pike said. "Cat got your tongues?"

When we still didn't speak, he walked in front of us, peering at our faces, and then squinted at the television. *The Rocky and Bullwinkle Show* was on, and he snorted and said, "That stuff will rot your brains," and lumbered on back to the kitchen.

We gave each other proud, anxious looks.

When our mother called "Supper's ready!" an hour later, we squared our shoulders and went into the dining room, where we'd only ever eaten before on holidays. Pike was parked at the head of the table. Alvin and I sat to his left, with Julie across from us.

Our mother had cooked a chicken, and she brought a platter of sliced white meat, thighs and drumsticks in and put it in the middle of the table with the other serving dishes, taking the chair beside Julie.

Pike asked us to bow our heads, which was something new. We'd always gone to church on Sunday, like everybody else in Baxter, but had never been overtly religious at home, while he was one of those people who make a point out of showing how devout they are.

He mumbled one of those *Lord, we thank thee for thy bounty* prayers, and my mother said, "Amen," and then Pike rubbed his hands together and grinned. I can see him now, wearing a white shirt with the sleeves rolled up on his hairy forearms.

"All right, troops!" he said. "Let's dig in!"

We didn't respond, and he gave us another speculative look. But then he shrugged and reached for a slice of white meat and a helping of mashed potatoes. He put a slab of butter on the potatoes and a heap of peas next to the potatoes, then passed the peas to Alvin.

We took silent turns with the various serving dishes.

While I was ladling peas onto my plate I felt Pike staring. I looked up and he was chewing with a lump in his cheek, watching my face. He held up a finger while he swallowed and the lump went away.

"So, Cal old pal," he said then. "What does a man do around this establishment for fun?" He raised his bottle of Budweiser, one finger around its neck, and took a slug.

"I don't know."

I slid my eyes over to Alvin, who was into his usual routine of arranging peas atop his mashed potatoes, making a pattern of three-pea triangles.

"Well, what about fishing?" Pike said. "Help me out here, son. You like to go fishing, don't you? That's a good-looking boat out there in the barn."

"That's our father's boat."

"Well, yeah. But a boat needs to be in the water."

I looked at my food, then back at him.

He raised one eyebrow and turned to Alvin.

"All right, what about Big Al? You must like fishing, don't you? Or hunting? You're a Maine boy, aren't you? All these fields, I bet there's woodcock around."

Alvin—who hated to be called *Al,* let alone *Big Al*—said, "I don't know, maybe," then went back to messing with his peas and potatoes.

Pike looked at our mother. He rotated the beer bottle by its neck on the table, and it made a sound like a big coin settling from a spin. Then he said, "Well," drawing it out, and turned to Julie. "What about Miss Skinny Minnie, then? Are you gonna talk to me?"

Julie just looked at her plate.

"Julia . . . " our mother said.

"Never mind, Betty, I think I get the picture." Pike looked around at us. "So that's how it is, huh? A little uprising by the termites? A little mutiny on the *Bounty*?"

"I'm sorry, Randy." My mother was frowning.

Pike waved a hand. "Tell you what, I don't normally have much use for rude kids, but maybe just this once we'll let it go, seeing as how this is such a big change and all."

"I don't know what's gotten into them."

Pike waved her off again, then leaned forward, pointing at us with his fork.

"That's today, termites," he said, and he was grinning, but the grin—bristly mustache, lots of teeth—was more fierce than friendly. "Today you get a pass, so get it all out of your systems."

"Well?" my mother said.

Alvin mumbled something that sounded like "I guess so," and I said, "Okay." Julie only cleared her throat, but Pike let that go, and with a satisfied sort of grunt and a scoop-and-stuff bite of mashed potatoes, let us know that the meal should resume.

While we were eating he told our mother he'd sold a house that morning to a customer he'd thought they'd lost after one of her botched attempts.

"I'm glad to hear that, Randy."

Then we were done, and my mother went for the apple pie she'd made earlier—she wasn't much for baking, so this was special—and we had pie and ice cream, and then we cleared the table.

In the kitchen Pike leaned against the stove with his hands in his pockets, watching us set everything down and our mother run hot water into the sink. Then he said, "You know what? Let's hold off on those dishes. Everybody into the living room."

He walked off in that direction.

My mother dried her hands on a dish towel.

"You heard him," she said, and nodded toward the hallway.

In the living room we sat on the couch and she took the high-backed chair next to us. Pike was arranging crumpled newspaper and kindling on the brick hearthstone. He built a tent over the kindling with small lengths of pine, then opened the damper and lit the paper. When it caught he put a bigger pine slab on top of the flames.

He put the screen back in place, perched on our father's recliner, and looked at the three of us on the couch.

"So let's hash this out," he said. "I'll work with you guys, okay? But you have to get with the program. And you need to know this straight up: I've never yet lived in a house where the kids were in charge, and I'm not about to start now. Okay?"

Alvin and I nodded.

Julie wouldn't look at him.

Pike pushed against his knees and stood. He stuck out his hand. I wasn't brave enough not to shake, and neither was Alvin. Julie still wouldn't look at him, though, so Pike just snatched her hand out of her lap, pumped it up and down and then set it back.

"There now," he said.

Julie tucked the hand under her arm.

That made Pike frown, but he just gave her a look, nodded at our mother, and said, "I'll let you talk amongst yourselves," and strode out of the room. We heard him cross the kitchen—he made the floor creak—and open the door. Then we heard the door bang shut.

The fire snapped in the fireplace and a swirl of sparks flew up the chimney.

Julie looked at our mother and said, "You're really in love with *him?*"

"Don't be rude, Julia."

"But you are? Like you were with Daddy?"

"Your father and I were very young when we got married. The war had just ended, too. With Mr. Pike, it's different. It's more like we're partners. We just want to make life a little easier for ourselves."

Nothing about us, her kids.

"Couldn't you do that without getting married?" Julie asked.

"Not really. Now listen to me: We all miss your father, but we should be grateful to Mr. Pike. It's not easy for a man to start up with a new family and take on someone else's problems."

"So you're marrying him for his money?"

I thought my mother might jump up and slap her. Julie looked like she was expecting it too and didn't care. But then our mother just stood, smoothed her dress over her hips, and walked out of the room.

We heard her go outside to the porch, and after looking at each other we walked single file around the corner, through the hallway, and into the kitchen. The light was on over the still-sudsy sink, but through the reflection in the window we could see her in the rocker, and in the gloom we saw the cigarette ember move toward her face and away.

"I'm not living here with that . . ." Julie stopped and hugged herself. I looked at her to see what she meant, and she stared back at me.

"That what?" Alvin said.

Julie just turned and walked out of the room. We set off after her.

In the living room she snapped on the TV. We'd missed one of our favorite shows, thanks to Pike, but it was always possible to find something to watch.

As the show progressed, though, I had only the sketchiest idea of what was happening to secret agent John Drake. I was too busy wondering—like Julie—how someone who was not only beautiful but had been married to our father could ever *join forces* with a phony like Randy Pike.

It really didn't make a lot of sense.

Of course, when you're ten going on eleven and your father has died and your world has turned upside down, there's a lot that doesn't make any sense.

TWELVE

Baxter, Spring, 1965

Little John Ladleigh was our local justice of the peace, and my mother married Randy Pike at his equally small house on Water Street, where the river narrowed and turned upstream toward the old iron bridge.

Pike wanted a church wedding, but his minister was away on a mission, and he thought the stand-in was prissy. So they went the JOP route, with the understanding that they'd try to have a proper church ceremony after the minister returned.

Ladleigh's little parlor was packed. We kids were there, of course, and Pike's parents and siblings, who all lived in Baxter, along with Pike's employees, a few fellow Realtors, and other local merchants.

It could have been even more crowded, though.

My Shaw grandparents weren't there. They'd never had much use for Pike—those jailbait rumors hadn't helped—and didn't feel that marrying their son's widow made him a legitimate member of their family. So they'd stayed home in Bath.

Uncle Gus had begged off, too. He claimed he couldn't abandon his Saturday music students, but actually, he was still embarrassed that my mother had turned down his own stammering and red-faced proposal, after she'd flunked out of job number two. ("Oh Gus," she'd said in her merciless way, "you can barely keep the wolf from the door as it is.")

And my mother's parents weren't there. She'd been glad to get away from them and come to Maine with Jack Shaw, and they'd never really reconciled. They were old, too—my mother had been an unwelcome surprise in their late forties—and not in good-enough health to make the trip from California anyway.

So there were plenty of missing people.

But it was still overcrowded, and with all those people so close I had to shut my eyes and breathe deeply, so as not to feel sick, and they were still shut when Ladleigh said, "Speak now or forever hold your peace."

I looked then to see if anyone would speak, but no one did, although Julie sat up straight and looked like she wanted to. So Ladleigh pronounced them man and wife, and Pike bent my mother over and kissed her. ("Ugh," Julie whispered then, and I felt even sicker to see him handling her like that. He was so much bigger and stronger, and I saw all at once that he could do whatever he wanted with her.) Then he pulled her upright again—she did her best to smile—and grinned out at the guests, who gave them a round of applause.

When the clapping trailed off, Pike slapped his paw into Ladleigh's hand and gave him a manly handshake that threw the little man off balance. Then he said, "Let's hear it for the bride!" and everyone cheered, and all the noise brought the swirls back to me, and I had to shut my eyes again. (It was all coming clear to me how much things were going to change. This guy was actually coming home with us. He would be there every night, and he would be sleeping in the same bed with my mother and putting his hands on her whenever he wanted.)

There was a lot of shuffling around, chairs moving and people talking. Then Alvin knocked me lightly on the head and said, "Earth to Calvin—everyone's leaving."

Outside in the cool air off the river I felt a little better. But there was a gauntlet of people throwing rice that we had to walk through on our way to the car. Someone had written *Just Married!* in soap on the back window of Pike's car, and there were tin cans tied to the back bumper with string that clattered as we drove off.

I hated all of it.

We kids were squeezed into the backseat. I opened my eyes just enough to watch him clap a hand on my mother's knee and grin. We paraded slowly through town to his apartment over the real estate office to pick up a suitcase, and I wondered what my mother thought about being on display like that; it was all so contrary to how she usually liked things.

When we got back to our house—his too, now, I realized again—the driveway was full of cars and pickups, and people were drinking beer on the porch.

Somebody's kids were swinging on the swing so hard that I thought they might break it, and I wanted to order them off but didn't know if I had the right anymore.

In the kitchen it was noisy and a little rowdy. Pike's two brothers each had a Budweiser in one hand and were trading shoulder slugs with the other, and when Pike came within reach they punched him, too, and he roared and returned the favor.

One of them saw me watching and feinted toward me with a grin. When I flinched he laughed and messed my hair the same way Pike did when he was pretending to be playful.

I didn't like it any better from him.

I joined Alvin and Julie, who were standing at the foot of the stairway, watching Pike give his fellow Realtors a tour of the upstairs, pointing out things that needed fixing: dings in the drywall, separated pieces of trim (which pissed me off, because I took it as criticism of my father).

They went into the big bedroom and one of them said, "Aha, the playroom!" and there were hoots and then Pike said, "Now, boys, none of that!"

Beside me Julie said again, "Ugh."

Next Pike walked everybody down to the boys' room and tossed open the door and his cronies stuck their heads in for a look.

Alvin whispered, "Jeezus."

They came out of our room and went to Julie's, and when Pike opened her door, Julie hissed under her breath and stalked away toward the kitchen.

"Where's she going?"

"How should I know?" Alvin still had his eyes trained upstairs.

Pike and his gang tramped back to the stairway, and we retreated to the kitchen.

Our mother was trapped in a corner by Pike's sister, who wore jeans and a checkered hunting shirt and was explaining how lucky our mother had been to land such a wonderful hunk of man.

"Excuse me," our mother said. "Yes, children?"

"We're looking for Julie," Alvin said.

"Oh. I think she went outside." She sounded disappointed, as if she'd been hoping we'd give her a reason to ditch the sister. But now she fell back, smiling grimly.

We grabbed our jackets and went outside. It was still cool, but the sun—which had warmed some lately—felt good on my face. I looked across our field past the old bare-limbed apple orchard to the river and saw that the ice sheets had retreated almost all the way to the shady riverbanks.

We walked down the driveway past all the vehicles, and Alvin pointed at the barn and said, "Bet she's in there," and we ran over to the side door, crossing a snow-patched bit of lawn.

I pulled the door shut behind us and we walked past the old box stalls to the wide drive bay. We crossed the bay to the open haymow, but Julie wasn't there, sprawled in the loose hay, where you'd sometimes find her reading.

"Hayloft?" I said.

Alvin looked up. The hayloft was a high platform way up near the barn roof supported by huge upright timbers, and from the middle two beams, parallel and three feet apart, it ran across the bay to a door high up on the wall. My father had told us that was where the conveyer used to go that moved bales back and forth, but the flooring and the conveyer were both long gone.

"Go check it out," I said.

"Why don't you?" Alvin smirked, because it was something he had over me. I'd fallen out of a pine tree when I was five, and it had taken a week for the headaches to go away. I'd been timid about heights ever since. That didn't stop me from playing in the hayloft, but I wasn't anxious to climb up that ladder if I didn't have to.

When I didn't say anything, he laughed and started up the ladder. But he stopped a couple of rungs up and looked back at me. I'd heard it, too: a rustling, as the feral cats that lived in the barn ran off to hide. We knew that meant Julie couldn't have gone up, because they'd have already hidden. (The cats had come with the house, and our father had never had the heart to get rid of them, not even when they stalked the swallows. He claimed they kept the barn rat-free, which was worth the occasional dead bird.)

He jumped down and we looked around again.

"There she is." Alvin pointed toward our father's boat—a twelve-foot Leavens Brothers, sitting on its aluminum trailer—where I could see Julie sitting on the middle seat.

We walked over.

Julie had on our father's old fly-fishing hat with the floppy brim and the dry flies stuck into the band. Her hair fell down out of the hat onto her shoulders, and she had his pipe in her mouth and one of his paperbacks cradled against her heart.

She'd been crying; her cheeks were shiny.

When we came up she took the pipe out of her mouth, held the book up, and said, "This is where he stopped reading." It was a Heinlein book—*Stranger in a Strange Land*—which I hadn't read, although I wanted to now.

"He was reading these words." Julie hugged the book again, and the sorrow in her voice blossomed in my own skull. Then she broke down, and I didn't know what to do except climb into the boat with her. Alvin did, too, and we sat silently in the bow (him) and stern (me)—slowly slipping down to sprawl against the gunnels—until she sniffled and laughed and said, "Remember the alligator in the toilet?"

We all laughed, remembering when our mother, in the act of sitting, had looked down to see a rubber gator googling up at her and had let out a scream of terror, and how it had taken her a week to speak to our father again.

We took turns telling other stories. It was a huge relief to talk about him with no one else around, and once we got started we didn't want to stop. It felt almost like he was back, and we were safe again.

But then we had to stop, because the double doors rattled suddenly, then squealed back on their rollers, and in the harsh bright sunlight our new stepfather came swaggering in with his cronies to show off his newly acquired barn.

"The bones are still pretty good," he told them as they stepped inside, "but she needs about ten coats of paint."

STILL ON
THE WAGON

THIRTEEN

Tampa, 1995

I make it back to the Dearborne Trailer Park around one a.m., and drag my weary ass down the center lane—past beat-up, chevron-spaced trailers—to the far end, where my seedy little home sits next to the scrub brush.

I try to walk quietly, thinking of sleeping kids, but I'm not sure it really matters anymore. Their trailer still has that empty feel, and I think again that they might have moved on, which makes me wonder what their new home might be like. I hope it gets better for them instead of worse.

At the same time, though, I wish they were still around, because I'll miss doing magic tricks for them. (I was working on a new one that involved moving a cotton ball mysteriously through a stack of paper cups.)

But then I remember I'm not going to be around either, because I've decided I'm going back to Maine, and since I don't want to pay rent while I'm away, I'm going to have to let my little tin paradise go.

Inside I slide the cornet case against the wall and flop down on the fold-out. Tired as I am I'm not ready to sleep, so I lie there trying to figure out what I have to do to get my ducks in a row before I leave.

It's not that much: settle with my landlord, let El Gordo know and talk to my probation officer. Go to Goodwill and drop off paperbacks, my old portable typewriter, pots and pans, extra clothes, see if I can pick up some kind of a travel bag. (My father's old navy duffel is still in New York, possibly at the apartment of a waitress I'd met at the Blue Note.)

So only a day or two. Then I'll take an overnight Greyhound to Portland. I'll sleep on the way, go straight to Maine Medical, see what's happening with Uncle Gus and when the time is right, call Alvin for a ride back to the old homestead.

Or maybe not; I'm not sure I want to be trapped in a car with Alvin for an hour, while he tries to get "caught up" on my recent history. Alvin can be relentless, and I do have options—have spent enough time on the road to consider myself a master hitchhiker, for one thing.

But I'll get home somehow. I can't go to Maine and not go home. How long I stay will depend on how many ghosts are around, and how bothersome they get.

Because I know there'll be ghosts.

I hit my little tin bathroom, then brush my teeth. The tingle in my lips reminds me that I played pretty well tonight, and that gets me thinking again about my new piece of music.

I take the horn and stick my fingers in the bell to mute it, not expecting much, but open to anything. Because sometimes if you take yourself by surprise and just start playing, it gives you a different angle.

I sit on the fold-out, aim the horn down between my knees, and play, cruising quietly into what I already have, swinging up to where I left off, hearing piano chords (in Red's rolling style) in the background. Then I jump to a place that works as far as scale and key, but just feels too ordinary.

I try something else, and that doesn't work either.

But I keep trying, and then something nudges me just a half-step modal, and that leads me in a direction I'm not expecting, and I go out there a ways and manage to find my way back, and brother, when I do, it raises the hair on my neck.

I hold still a moment, feeling it.

I play it again and it still moves me, and once more, and this time the name drops into view. It comes to me about two bars past that new half-step departure: pale blue letters splashed across a blonde contour that is the shape of everything I know about this piece so far.

"Blue Summer" is the name, and as I take that half step once more, it gets darker and more settled, and the shape curves around on itself and then snakes back through, and I'm past the new part and back to the melody.

It gets me all the way up to the coda before I'm stuck again.

I play it a couple more times and I'm still stuck there so I give it a rest. I don't write anything down, trusting the shape of it, trusting that if any of it does happen to fall away, it'll be because it needed to.

When the rapping comes on my door and I check my watch, I'm amazed to find that it is three-thirty in the morning. Suddenly, then, I feel very sleepy.

I cradle the Olds and wait. The knocking gets louder and more rhythmic, someone pattering with the knuckles of both hands, and I wait for them to wear themselves out and leave, so I can lie down and let "Blue Summer" carry me off.

Then I hear, "Yo, Calvin!" and another thump, and I realize it's Kincaid, and I nearly shuffle over to open the door just so I can see if Celeste Boucher is with him. But I really don't have the energy. He'll have a bottle with him and I don't want to be tested. I'm still on the wagon and I want to stay there, and I want to take "Blue Summer" to bed.

So I stay put, and eventually Kincaid gives up and leaves; I hear the doors slam on his Supra and his tires squawk on the pavement as he drives off.

FOURTEEN

Tampa, 1995

It's nearly 4:30 a.m. when I finally shut off the lights and lie down on my little bed. And tired as I feel, now that I'm ready to call it a day, I wonder if I'll be able to. Sometimes the more tired you feel, the harder it is to get to sleep.

But I need to at least rest, so I stretch out under my old green blanket, figuring to just lie still and see what happens. Eventually the trailer park will come alive, and if I'm still awake by then, I figure I'll give up and roll out of bed and see if I have the energy to start on my errands.

Turns out I shouldn't have worried. I guess the long day caught up with me, because as soon as I put my head down I'm dead to the world. And I stay that way, right through the morning, and might have slept even longer if a neighbor didn't decide to goose his backfiring jalopy just outside my door.

The racket brings me back, but not all the way. You know how it is when you're jolted out of a deep sleep. I don't quite know where I am, because I've been dreaming about home—I'm sure "Blue Summer" took me there—and that still feels real, and for the moment I can't reconcile it with either the backfiring car or the cramped space around me.

I'm not in my bedroom, or anywhere else in the farmhouse, which doesn't make sense, because I was about to sneak out and make a dash to the barn, where Julie was waiting.

I was plotting how to get there without alerting Pike, so he wouldn't trail after me and give us a hard time (one of his main sources of recreation). Only just now I can't figure out which way to go.

The doorway to the cellar seems to be missing, so I can't steal out that way. And there's no side door that lets you sneak between two blue spruce trees and sprint—like a soldier running for cover—for the barn's side door.

Everything is different, and the damn noisy car is making it hard to think, and finally I kneel up on the bed and look out the window.

It's overcast and gray. Everything is paved, and there's no river, and a battered old Ford is stopped at a cross lane, trying not to stall, smoke roiling up from its exhaust.

Slowly, I come to recognize the trailer park, and the Ford as belonging to the double-wide three spots away, and as soon as that happens my head clears as if a damper has been opened. I'm back in the here and now.

The Ford revs one last time and sputters down the lane, and when it turns onto Dearborne I sink down away from the window. It hurts to be yanked back into the real world, where people you just dreamed about are gone all over again. It hurts to be this stumble-bum fool and not the kid in my dream, even if the kid in the dream had plenty of his own pain.

It gets worse as I sit there, a deep, lonesome ache, and I think how I'd give anything to go back to when I still had Julie, to be able to scramble out to that barn, to slip in through the side door past the cow stalls and climb (timidly) up to the hayloft, where she would be sitting on an old bale of hay, eyes shining in the dim light.

But unfortunately I'm all the way awake now, and I realize there are thirty years and far too many troubles between me and any such possibility.

PRINCESSES
DON'T CRY

FIFTEEN

Baxter, Spring, 1966

That wasn't the first time I dreamed about Julie and the barn. Not by a long shot. And when I did, it wasn't unusual for Pike to stick his ugly nose into the picture. After all, he was the reason we started hiding out there in the first place, because he wouldn't leave Julie alone.

See, Julie steadfastly refused to accept Pike as part of the family, and he couldn't handle it. Everybody else was on board to some degree— my mother *had* to pretend he was all right, and Alvin proved to be pretty flexible, and once the whole *joining forces* thing was a done deal, I have to admit to taking the path of least resistance—but that didn't matter, because in Pike's world, things had to be unanimous. So when he became convinced that Julie wouldn't warm up on her own, it only followed that he'd try to make it happen.

At first this was only creepy, because he thought he could charm her into changing her mind. He'd sit down in the living room while she was practicing and nod his head or snap his fingers (off-beat, of course). We'd be getting ready to head outside for the bus and he'd make some inappropriate remark about how nice she looked ("The boys are gonna like that little dress!"). He'd trap her into conversations about how school was going, or what she might be reading ("Nancy Drew, huh? I used to read those Tom Swift books when I was a kid!"), and he'd lean close to pester her at the table: "Can I reach you some more peas, sweetheart?"

Sometimes he'd put his arm around her and walk her from one room to another, or take her by the shoulders and jostle her lightly, as if to jolly her out of her "mood."

Julie hated all of this, of course, and would shrink away from him, and dodge him when she could, and in general make it obvious that she wanted to be left alone.

But Pike wasn't someone who could take a hint. And our mother was no help; she maintained that if Julie would only meet him halfway, everything would work itself out. So things went on this way, with Pike getting more and more "charming," and Julie, more and more resistant, and then one day he crossed the line and blew everything up.

I remember it was early spring, and Pike had been living with us for nearly a year. The bus had dropped us off after school and we'd come kicking up the driveway through wet, brown leaves that the retreating snow had left behind. We'd walked into the kitchen to find Pike waiting, obviously with some new angle concerning Julie from the way he jumped up from the table—where he'd been sitting with our mother—and took my sister by the arm.

"Have I got a deal for you!" he said, and launched into this "amazing" idea he'd had to have her play the piano at the open house he was planning for the real estate office that coming Saturday.

"We're gonna have hors d'oeuvres and all that, and I'm gonna have an upright brought in so you can play some of that longhair stuff." (It wasn't really longhair that Julie loved best, but forties and fifties standards, the stuff my father used to play, but Pike didn't know the difference.) "Give the old place some class, right? So what do you say?"

He turned her loose and stood there beaming.

Julie rubbed her arm, said, "No thank you," and cut for the stairs, walking like someone who doesn't quite dare to run. But maybe she should have run, because before she made it out of the room Pike had taken three long steps and cut her off.

"Oh no you don't," he said, grinning as if they were playing some sort of consensual game.

They stood looking at each other, and then Julie made a move to slip past him, and Pike—amazingly—hooked a shoulder into her midsection, grabbed her across the bottom and hoisted her up. Then he carried her right back to the table and set her down, dusting his hands and saying, "Don't think you're getting out of it that easy, sweetheart!"

Julie yanked her dress back into place. Her face was bright red, and she looked beseechingly at our mother. But when all our mother did was say, "Oh, Randy, now you've embarrassed her," she cried out wordlessly and bolted from the room. We heard her running up the stairs, and then her door slamming shut.

Pike looked at our mother. "What's her problem?"

"You shouldn't pick her up like that, Randy."

"Like what?"

"Like she's a little kid."

"She *is* a little kid."

"She's almost fifteen now. She's a young lady."

"Give me a break."

"I know you mean well . . ."

"What's that supposed to mean?" Pike said. Then he waved a hand and said, "Forget it," and yanked the door open and lumbered outside.

Our mother sighed.

Alvin looked at me and shrugged as if to say *The show's over.*

"Come on," he said, and headed for the doorway.

In the living room we sat down on the sofa and I said, "Jeez, he picked her up like a sack of potatoes."

"Oh, he's just not used to having kids."

"That's no excuse."

"According to Mum it is."

Alvin sounded like he believed her. But he'd been thawing toward Pike, had even gone down to the river with him to try out a batch of new lures once the ice went out of the river. I thought he'd made up his mind—in his calculating way—to become the favorite stepson. (Which was fine with me at the time—I certainly didn't want the honor—but which before long would only help to make Pike a more-confident tyrant.)

We sat on the sofa and pretty soon he was watching the tube like an addict, with his mouth open. I couldn't settle down, though, because no matter what Alvin said, I knew something bad had happened, and didn't have any idea what to do about it.

I didn't know what to do later, either, when after a few weeks Pike gave up trying to win Julie over and switched instead to showing her just who was boss. This was a mean and deliberate change that Alvin's double cross and our mother's willful blindness helped make possible. It freed up the truly ugly side of Pike's nature, and brought a sense of dread into our house that you could feel the way you feel electricity in the air.

Pike had basically declared war on my sister. But he maintained the phony cheer, pretending that he was just using humor like anyone might if they were at the end of their rope with a recalcitrant child. (This allowed our mother to keep pretending that everything was hunky-dory.)

He started calling her Princess instead of sweetheart, and merrily vetoing overnights at Becky O'Dell's, and sending her outside "for some fresh air" when she wanted to practice.

Sometimes he'd make a point out of fondling our father's personal property—golf clubs or guns, the boat, his fishing gear—knowing how much that would bother her.

"This is one sweet rifle," he said one day, bringing Dad's .30-30 out to where Julie and I were reading on the porch swing. "Bambi's in trouble now!" He levered it, sighted on a squirrel, and dry-fired (something our father always told us never to do, because it wore down the mechanism). Then he raised his eyebrows and grinned at us.

He'd "tease" (badger) her about how well she was doing her chores. One such chore was washing the dishes, and on another day I was spying from the hallway while he loomed over her and examined every plate and glass as she finished washing them, setting many of them back in the dishwater and saying, "That one's no good," or "Nope, still dirty," until it was finally too much and she started to cry, which had obviously been his intent from the beginning. It was awful to watch and made me want to punch him.

"Come on, now," he said. "Princesses don't cry."

Which made her cry harder, and when she couldn't stop, it gave him an excuse to take her by the arm, turn her toward the doorway, and march her out of the kitchen.

"Go on up to your room," he said, releasing her at the foot of the stairs.

He stood with his hands on his hips watching her make her way up.

When the coast was clear—Pike had gone outside—I ran upstairs, thinking to try and comfort Julie somehow. But I didn't, because I couldn't figure out what to say or do. So I turned into my own room instead of hers and sat on my bunk. I stewed about Pike's bullying for an hour.

And that night is when I finally decided to get involved.

Pike had gone to town for a meeting of some sort and I tracked my mother down in the basement, where she was doing the laundry. When I told her what had happened, she said, "He just wants things done right," and kept right on pulling the wet clothes out of the washer into a basket.

It was the sort of thing she always said, but I wasn't going to let her get away with it this time.

"He picks on her all the time now."

"Oh, I wouldn't call that picking on her."

"Well, I would."

"He's tried and tried to be nice to that girl."

"He just pretends to be nice."

"Why would he pretend?"

"To fool you."

She didn't like that, and stopped with the clothes. "I think that's quite enough, Cal."

"You have to do something."

"You go on back upstairs."

"No," I said.

"Don't tell me no, Calvin Shaw."

She wasn't going to listen any more than she ever did, and I glared at her, drew my foot back, and kicked the side of the washing machine.

She looked open-mouthed at me. "What has gotten into you?"

"Nothing!"

"You get upstairs or I'm calling your stepfather right now. Then he'll come home and you can take it up with him."

We stared at each other, and I was going to cry if I didn't do something, so I whirled away and stomped back up the stairs. I kicked the door shut, good and loud, so she'd be sure to hear. It was weak, though, because what I seriously wanted to do was kick her, for choosing Pike over Julie.

I went looking for Julie. She wasn't in her room. I checked the living room, where Alvin was watching a soap opera.

"Where's Julie?" I said, and when he just looked at me and said, "How should I know," I went out onto the porch and found her in the swing, sitting with her legs tucked under.

She was holding a book but not reading, just staring out at the yard. When I shut the kitchen door she looked at me, and when I walked toward her she moved over.

I sat down and pushed off against the floorboards to get us moving, and while we rocked I told her about complaining to our mother, and how far it had gotten me. I wanted her to know I was on her side.

Julie's eyes were shiny in the low light.

"Don't bother, Cal," she said, and there was a hitch in her voice. "She'll never listen."

"Why not?"

"She doesn't care about us anymore."

"She's still our mother."

"She's Mrs. Pike now, and that's all she wants to be."

We rocked quietly for a minute or two.

"Then who's going to help?" I said.

She looked across the yard at the river. "Nobody."

"Maybe Nanny and Grampa Shaw might."

"Are you going to walk down to Bath?"

"How about Uncle Gus, then?"

She laughed bitterly. "You know he's scared of Pike."

"What are we gonna do then?"

"Nothing. They don't let kids do anything."

"We have to do something."

"We can grow up," she said, and her eyes narrowed as if she were looking three or four years down the road, when she'd be old enough to do what she wanted.

I didn't know what else to say. I was still upset, but proud, too, that she'd spoken as if we were in it together. It was the start of us getting closer. Always before she'd been just an older sister—three years was a lot—and someone I admired from a distance.

Julie opened her book: a Nancy Drew.

I kicked at the floorboards, and we swung and she read and the chains creaked. I looked up at where they hung on hooks from the porch ceiling. Then the eaves with their old phoebe nests caught my eye.

The eaves were like little cubbies at the end of the slanted porch joists, and phoebes were always trying to build nests there, but it never seemed to work out. Something always scared them off or killed them. I could see three of the unfinished nests now, tucked sadly into the corners.

I sat with Julie until the sun dropped below the trees and it cooled off. Then I hopped off the swing and Julie did too and we went back into the house. She set off up the stairs for her room, but I headed for the piano. Saying Uncle Gus's name had reminded me that I had to practice. It was Saturday, and we had lessons tomorrow, and I hadn't put in the time I should have during the week.

I liked lesson day with Uncle Gus, and with everything going on in our house, it would feel like an escape to go there. Although I was never much for practicing (until I took up the trumpet, anyway), I wanted to make sure I held up my end of the bargain now, so nobody would decide it should end.

SIXTEEN

Baxter, Spring, 1966

Uncle Gus's studio was in the basement of his little ranch house. Pike would drop us off there on the way back from church—he insisted the whole family go and listen to the Word of God—and after our lessons we would walk home along the River Road.

Pike would park in front of Uncle Gus's one-car garage and say "Out you go." He didn't really like that we took lessons there and was always churlish about dropping us off. I thought it was because Uncle Gus had been my father's best friend, and was a living reminder of our life before Pike showed up. But the lessons were free, and he hadn't come up with a plausible reason to stop us yet.

We'd jump out and walk in our church clothes to the side door with its little porch. Inside, Uncle Gus would be making coffee, listening to jazz on the stereo system he had set up on the credenza in his living room. (The stereo was one of his few extravagances, another being a Martin Committee trumpet like the one his hero Clark Terry played.)

"Go on down," he'd say. "Be right with you."

He'd divided the basement into two sections—one with the furnace and water heater, and one he'd finished with that fake-pine paneling that everyone used back then, and by laying down shag carpeting. There was an easy chair on one side, adjacent to the piano, where he sat with his coffee and cigarette. The only natural light came from narrow cellar windows, so he'd added a couple of fluorescent fixtures, one at each end.

Across from his chair were three student-type desks he'd salvaged from somewhere, and at the far end of the room were his other instruments on stands—trumpet, trombone, saxophone, clarinet—and a cabinet where he kept supplies of music books, reeds, and mouthpieces.

Some of the wall panels weren't flush, and he hadn't put a mopboard down to hide the carpet edges, and you could tell a professional hadn't put in the drop ceiling (which was yellowed above his chair from cigarette smoke), but I thought it was a fine room anyway, because it was all about music.

Uncle Gus would start off with our homework. But he wasn't intense about it, and there were no real consequences if you hadn't studied and practiced. (If I hadn't studied, I should say; Alvin always had his done, and Julie didn't have to study. Uncle Gus would look sadly at me when I was unprepared, would say something like "I don't want you to work on the scales for me, Cal, I want you to work on them for *you*," and I would feel guilty and do better for the next week or two.)

Next, we'd take turns playing.

I always led off, then Alvin would have a go, and finally Julie would finish. Uncle Gus liked saving her for last, because while I had some keyboard talent and Alvin wasn't bad, Julie was amazing.

She played elegantly, with her hands moving gracefully up and down, as if she also made ethereal music in the space above the keys. (Sometimes they would linger there until you would think she couldn't possibly get them back to the keys in time, but she always managed.)

"Young lady," Uncle Gus would say, "you have a gift."

After we played he would discuss how we'd done, and then would stub out his cigarette and go to the piano and play our assignments himself, for clarity. (He was a trumpeter, but always said he could get by with any instrument that didn't have strings. I thought that he did much better than "get by" on the piano, though; he was actually pretty good.) Then he would set the cover down over the keys and the lesson would be over.

We'd go upstairs and he would drive us home if it was raining or snowing, but otherwise nobody thought anything of us hiking that couple of miles back to the house. We'd walk on the river side, where there was a well-trod path through the tall pines. We'd take our time and talk about the lesson and maybe make affectionate fun of Uncle Gus's size or the way he talked, and we'd laugh and all feel pretty close walking along the river, even Alvin.

But that feeling of normalcy, the sense of respite we took from Uncle Gus's basement, only lasted until we passed the Old Settlers Cemetery, which was a cluster of vestigial gravestones from the colonial days in a pine grove, set off a few yards toward the water.

The cemetery was our halfway point, and meant we'd be home soon. That always put a damper on our high spirits. I remember we'd walk more slowly, as if to hold on to the good feeling as long as possible. But it wasn't as easy to talk and laugh, because we knew that when we got home, nothing would have changed: Pike would still pick on Julie; Alvin and my mother would still pretend everything was fine; Julie would resume her role as the unreasonably stubborn holdout against family unity.

And as for me?

I was in limbo for a while—taking that path of least resistance—but after my mother ratted me out about talking behind Pike's back, I quickly joined Julie on the official shit list.

SEVENTEEN

Baxter, Summer, 1966

Pike didn't waste any time confronting me.

He came into the living room, took me by the arm and hoisted me off the sofa, and then marched me out onto the porch. He pulled the kitchen door shut with a bang, held the screen door open with a foot while he swung me out of the way, and let it slap shut behind us.

Still holding me by the arm, he said, "So you've been sticking your nose in where it doesn't belong."

I hated my mother for betraying me. "She's my sister."

"So what?"

"So stop picking on her!" I yelled this at him, then wished I hadn't, because he squeezed my arm, hard, and brought his face down so close that I could smell his sour breath.

"You really want to start up with me?"

There was a meanness always lurking in Pike, and sometimes you could feel it bubbling up, like I did now. It wasn't something you wanted to trigger.

"No," I said.

"You're damn right you don't."

He held me there, daring me to say something else, but I'd used up my small store of courage and kept my mouth shut until he laughed his nasty laugh and shook me loose.

Afterwards I joined Julie in doing my best to avoid him. That worked sometimes, but not if he'd come looking for you because he felt like pushing somebody around.

He liked stiff-fingered shoves to get you moving, and taking you by the arm to walk you to your next chore. And there were always plenty of chores.

There were dirty floors, dusty corners, and smudged windows; grass that needed mowing and leaves to rake; and as long as you had the rake out, there was a driveway to smooth, and there was this, and there was that. And he was always deceitfully cheerful about it, which let our mother ignore the underlying bullying. (I was convinced by now that she would always be on his side, and you can't imagine how desolate that made me feel; or maybe you can.)

Sometimes Pike would have a red-letter day, when he found a way to harass both Julie and me at the same time. I remember one Saturday when we were sitting together on the porch swing reading (she was rereading her all time favorite: *The Wind in the Willows*; I had one of Dad's mythology books). We'd finished our chores and Pike had gone golfing—Dad's clubs rattling in the back of his pickup— and we'd thought we were in the clear.

But then he came back down the River Road, turned into the driveway, and skidded to a stop in front of the house, raising dust that drifted up onto the porch. He'd forgotten something—his wallet, maybe—and had had to about-face, and he wasn't happy about it. But when he climbed out of the pickup and saw us there—still swinging, books in our indolent laps, undeserved guilt on our faces—that displeasure gave way to a sort of heartless joy that you could easily read in his face.

He stood beside the pickup, big as a grizzly, golf polo stretched tight across his chest, and we stopped rocking and the swing swung shorter and then halted.

"Time on your hands, huh?" Pike crossed his arms and thought for a moment. Then he gave us one of his narrow-eyed smiles and pointed with his thumb over his shoulder. "Come with me."

He set off down the driveway. Then he called out: "Snap to it, termites!"

We slid off the swing and walked after him.

At the barn he shoved the double-door back and disappeared inside. We got there in time to see him lifting the boat trailer by its hitch. He leaned backwards, the muscles in his arms flexing, and slowly got the trailer moving. Then, taking quick little backward steps, he pulled it outside. He dropped the hitch and went back for the hose that was always coiled next to the spigot by the cow stalls.

Playing the hose out he walked back, then returned for a bucket and sponge and the bottle of vinegar/detergent mix left over from our father's last season with the boat. He set the bucket and bottle down on the grass in front of us.

"There," he said. "Now you're in business. Let's see how clean you can get this battleship."

He picked up the end of the hose and held it out to me.

"Why do we have to clean it?" I said.

Pike smiled, leaned forward, and tapped me on the head with the brass fitting on the end of the hose. "Because I'm telling you to."

I wanted to hit him back, and he could tell; he took a quick look at the house, then tapped me again. This time he hit a soft spot and I wanted so much to slug him in the mouth, but I didn't dare, so I just stood there and tried not to blink, because then he'd know my eyes were filling.

"Stop it," Julie said. "We'll do it."

Pike grinned and handed her the hose.

"I knew I could count on you, Princess!"

Then he went marching back up the driveway. He climbed inside his pickup, turned around on the grass, and drove back, still grinning out the window at us. He swung onto the River Road and headed off fast.

I rubbed my head. "Jerk!"

"Double jerk!" Julie said.

She went into the barn, turned on the water, then came back and dribbled some of the cleaner into the bucket and splashed water in from the hose. She dipped the sponge and got to work wiping the boat's hull. When she finished a section, I jetted it clean with a thumb over the hose.

We'd been working for a half-hour when I spotted Alvin sitting on the porch steps, his glasses glinting in the sunlight. When he saw me looking he got up and started down the driveway, hands in his chino pockets.

He came up and stood beside the boat.

"Join right in," I said.

"Thanks just the same."

Julie reached the stern and wiped that down and moved around to the other side. I followed with the hose, and it wasn't long before Alvin walked around to join us.

"All right, I'll take a turn."

Julie gave him the sponge and sat down on the wet grass, flexing her right arm. Alvin knelt on the weedy old hay-wagon tracks and started scrubbing in this wide-sweeping, showy way that he obviously thought was much better than what she'd been doing.

With the two of them switching off, and me following with the hose, it went faster.

Then Becky O'Dell came up the driveway on her bicycle—she'd ridden to town—and after she dropped her bike and hobbled over to pitch in, looking like Raggedy Ann in her blue jumper with her mop of red hair, we really made some time.

We were done with the hull before noon and sat down on the grass to take a break. I watched Becky claw her hair back and twist it into a ponytail, which she fixed in place with a rubber band. She hated her hair and was always trying to corral it somehow.

"There!" she said when she was done.

"Do you think we have to do the inside?" Julie asked.

"Better rinse it out at least," Alvin said. He got up and pulled the drain plug, and he and Becky—who was strong, like all the O'Dells—held the bow end of the trailer up so I could lean across the transom and hose it down, the water running out at my feet.

When it was done they let the trailer down and we stood back. It was nice to see the boat clean again. Pike and his brothers never even rinsed it; just stuck it in the barn.

"How come you're cleaning the boat, anyways?" Becky said. She was pretty in a tomboy sort of way, with her dark eyebrows and ice-blue eyes.

"It wasn't our idea," Julie said.

Becky looked at her. "Oh."

"Yeah," Julie said.

We shut the water off and Alvin drained the hose by holding it over his head and passing it through his hands while he walked across the drive bay. Some of the water dripped out behind him, but most of it ran out the other end.

We put the hose, the bucket, and the rest of the cleaning stuff away and went back out, climbing into the boat and arranging ourselves on its two forward seats (Alvin and Julie) and aft bench.

We sat there enjoying the sun and not talking. I was thinking about my father and how he'd take us upriver to town, how he'd tie up at the town dock and lead us up the hill to Main Street. He liked to make us laugh by pretending he was a tour guide, as if Baxter were some tourist Mecca. ("Now folks, this little park bench is the very spot where in 1958 Mr. Early Blake sold his first batch of illegal clams!")

After we'd been sitting in the boat for a couple of minutes, Becky, who could never still for long, said, "Hey, want to go up in the hayloft and make a fort?"

"Cal's scared of the hayloft."

"Shut up, Alvin."

"I don't want to anyway," Julie said.

"Want to come over to my house? I can use the outboard by myself, now." Becky sounded proud. "We can go fishing; the mackerel are running something wicked!"

"Is your father home?" Julie asked. (Becky's parents weren't much better than ours. Her father was a lobster fisherman who didn't like other people's kids, and we knew if he was home he'd find some reason to say no about the boat. Then if we played a board game or something he'd hang around looking annoyed until we gave up and went home.)

Becky said, "Okay, never mind."

"Sorry," Julie said.

"That's okay." She rocked onto a hip, got a leg under her, and stood up. "I guess I'll mosey along."

"Thanks for helping."

"No problem!" Becky put her arms around Julie—the only kid I knew who hugged other kids like that—and looked at me as if I might be next. But I said, "Oh no you don't," and she stuck out her tongue and limped over to her bike. (She didn't try with Alvin, and maybe he looked a little wistful about that, although it was hard to tell with him.)

We watched her coast down the driveway and lean onto the River Road—she looked normal riding a bike—and then we started back to the house.

"Well, that was fun," I said.

Alvin said, "I guess he gets a little carried away sometimes."

"You think?" Julie said.

We came up to the house.

"Maybe if you tried being nicer to him."

"Maybe he should try being nicer to us," Julie said.

"He can be half decent."

"To you, maybe."

"Yeah, to his little pal."

"Shut up, Cal."

We climbed the porch steps.

"You guys can't win against him anyway."

"He can't win against us, either." Julie opened the screen door.

"I don't know about that. You cleaned the boat."

"Shut up."

We went into the kitchen. Our mother, at the table, sipped from her coffee cup and turned a page of the newspaper over. "Was that Rebecca O'Dell I saw helping you clean the boat?"

"No, that was Raggedy Ann."

"Don't be smart, Calvin." She gave me a look that meant I shouldn't get too big for my britches again, or she'd tell Pike. I'd had a hard time not being smart with her since the laundry-room episode.

"Anyway, that was a nice thing, to help out like that."

"Uh-huh," Alvin said.

"It was nice of all of you to clean the boat."

"He told us to," Julie said.

"It was still a nice thing to do."

Julie looked at me. I shrugged.

We followed Alvin out of the kitchen and into the living room. He switched on the TV and we all sat on the couch. There was nothing really good on, but we sat there watching anyway until Pike came home.

We heard him in the kitchen, bragging about his golf game, and then he came hulking into the living room. You could tell he'd had a couple with the boys after his round; his cheeks always got pink when he drank.

"What the hell are you termites watching, cartoons?"

"Uh-huh," Alvin said. "The boat's all done."

"Good," Pike said.

"I went down and helped."

"Good for you."

Pike was staring at the TV. "We can do better than that garbage." He walked over to the TV and started switching through the channels.

When Julie and I got up to leave he smiled at us over his shoulder.

EIGHTEEN

Baxter, Fall, 1966

So that's how that spring and summer went, and then suddenly it was the first Saturday in September, just a few days before school was to start again. It was Saturday the fourth, actually; I know the exact date, because it was the worst day of my life, which is really saying something.

I've never been able to talk it about very well, and even typing it won't be easy, but there's no point in setting this all down if I shy away at this point.

Julie and I were alone in the house for once, because Pike had taken off fishing, and our mother had gone to pick up Alvin from the school science fair, where he'd won a prize for this little electric motor he'd made out of coils of wire, a bolt, and a battery.

We were watching *American Bandstand* (which Pike had banned as being sinful) and giggling while we twisted and turned on the couch, making fun of the city kids' dance moves.

Then something changed in the room and we stopped.

It was Pike, standing in the doorway, sunburned and red-eyed, wearing khaki shorts and a yellow Pike Agency sweatshirt, with the sleeves cut off. We hadn't heard him come in—because of the music, or because he could move very quietly when he wanted to; he liked to sneak up and see what he could catch you doing.

He just stared at us at first, then took two big steps over to the TV and snapped it off.

"Garbage," he said, and he was slurring just a bit.

He turned to see how we'd react, but Julie and I just got up from the sofa and headed for the hallway. If you didn't make a fuss and avoided interacting, it would sometimes be all right.

But this wasn't one of those times. I made the mistake of glancing back as we turned the corner—which narrowed Pike's eyes and pretty much drew him after us—and then when we were both in the hallway, Julie said, "God, I hate him."

She said it quietly, but two more stealthy strides had brought Pike close enough to hear. He barged into the hallway behind us and barked, "What's that?"

We felt his words like darts, and walked faster. But we didn't run, because it might provoke him even more. He caught us in the kitchen, brushing me out of the way and grabbing Julie by the arm. He turned her so they were face-to-face.

"Got something on your mind, Princess?"

Julie said, "No!" and tried to pull away, but Pike wouldn't let go. When she kept struggling, he took her under both arms and brought her face up close, giving her a shake in the process. "I asked you a question, missy!"

I couldn't breathe, the air was so charged. I couldn't move, either. But then Pike shook Julie again, and I jumped him. I threw my arms around his bull neck and yanked. But scrappy as I'd become lately, I was still just a skinny boy, and it was no trouble at all for him to twist and snap his shoulders and send me stumbling across the room into the kitchen table.

I slid to the floor and tried to cry out, but the table edge had knocked the wind out of me. I was gasping and then Pike was looming over me. I kicked out and caught him on the knee, and he hopped and growled and raised his fists.

But Julie screamed, "Stop it!" and that seemed to startle him. He lowered his fists and looked at her. His eyes were still slits and his teeth were bared, but maybe he realized that he was about to do something impossible to explain away.

He looked at me and said, "You get outside, now!"

I grabbed the tabletop and pulled myself up. My breath had come back in a rush, and scared as I was, I was also still looking to kick him again. He saw it in my face, and turned his hips defensively, waiting for me to try it. He was still right on the edge. But Julie saw it too and said, "Cal, don't—please."

It was the *please* that got me. I thought it meant that things would be better for her if I left, and worse if I didn't. I tried to keep an eye on Pike and look at her too, but it was hard, and then she said again, "Please, Cal."

So I said, "You better leave her alone," and started around Pike to the door. When he just looked at me he didn't seem so wild, and I thought that he wouldn't shake her again. He might bully her into crying, like with the dishes, but maybe the worst was over.

At the door I turned to watch Julie walk out of the kitchen, with Pike behind her. He said, "Get up to your room and shut the door," and then he came back into the kitchen to see what I was doing, so I went outside.

I sat on the porch swing to wait. It was a surprise to see it was still daylight, like coming out of a movie theater. I felt stunned and alone, and so helpless. I was scared and furious and didn't know what to do with myself. I wished I'd ignored Julie and attacked Pike again, even if he'd have beaten me into a bloody pulp. Only, who knows what he might have done to Julie then. I didn't care about myself, but that might have been worse for her.

It was so hard to know anything for sure.

I pounded my fists onto my knees and stood up from the swing and walked back and forth along the porch. Then I walked down the steps and around the side of the house to where I could look up at Julie's window. I couldn't see into her room, and I couldn't hear anything. I went back around the house to the porch and sat on the swing again, and a few minutes later, the door opened and Julie came out.

I jumped up. "Are you all right? What did he do?"

She said, "I want to go up to the hayloft," and set off down the steps without another word. When I caught up I heard her breathing in little gasps and I said again, "Are you all right?" but she didn't answer, just walked faster down the driveway.

We crossed the grass, entering the side door into the barn.

It had been bright outside, and for a moment we couldn't see. When our eyes adjusted we crossed the drive bay past the dirty-again boat and walked over to the hayloft ladder.

Julie said, "Go ahead," and I started climbing, and halfway up I heard the cats slipping away through the loose hay to hide among the bales.

NINETEEN

Baxter, Fall, 1966

We sat on our old, saggy bales in the dusty hayloft without talking. It was warm up there. Julie had stopped gasping but looked wilted and sad. She looked like I felt. It's completely demoralizing to have an angry man put his hands on you when you're just a kid, and it's even worse to have him put his hands on your sister.

Julie was staring at the hay door, outlined by leaking sunlight. Every now and then she'd sigh. There were dark emotions radiating out of her and billowing around the hayloft.

After a while we heard the side door creak open and we held still, thinking he'd come after us, wondering if he'd haul himself up the ladder.

But then we recognized the uneven footsteps. "Anybody in here?"

Julie looked at me.

It was Becky O'Dell, stopping in again, but neither of us wanted to see her just then, so we stayed quiet, and after a moment we heard her leave.

Limp-thump, limp-thump.

When she shut the door it got gloomy all over again in the barn. Julie was staring at the hay door. Then she stood up and walked to the edge of the platform, stopping there and looking over the edge at the long drop to the floor.

"What are you doing?"

"I'm going to walk it."

"You'd better not."

Her shoulders went up and down. "I've done it before."

"When?"

"Lots of times."

Just like that she stepped onto the two parallel timbers, one foot on each, and I got very queasy in the pit of my stomach. Then she started across. There was a two-foot gap between the timbers and she had to move each foot a few inches at a time, holding her arms out for balance.

My heart squeezed in on itself. I would no more have gone out there than I would have walked a tightrope over Niagara Falls. But Julie managed to shuffle all the way across. Then she hooked her hand over a board that had been nailed across two of the studs, reached with the other hand and turned the piece-of-wood latch that held the hay door shut. She leaned back to let the door open inward, then hung herself over the doorway and looked out at the driveway, the yard, and the river.

A breeze came past her into the barn, ruffling her hair.

She looked over her shoulder at me.

"What do you think you're doing?"

"What I want to do."

She turned back to look out the door. Then after a minute or two she slipped her hand behind the nailed board, leaned out of the way again, and pushed the door shut. She re-latched it, turned carefully and sat down on the beam.

"You better be careful!"

"I told you I've done it before."

"I never saw you."

"You weren't here."

Julie put her hands flat on the timber, took a peek over the side, then tipped her head back and tossed her head. "You wouldn't understand, Cal."

"Maybe I would."

"I don't think so."

I sat still and didn't say anything.

"All right," she said. "I do it because nobody can tell me not to, okay? Nobody can stop me or make me do something else."

"You mean Pike?"

She shut her eyes. "Anybody."

"All right. Will you please come back now?"

"In a minute. Turn around first and don't look."

"Why?"

"Just do it."

"Tell me why, first."

"Please, Cal?"

Since she said *please* I turned around. But then I cocked my head to look at her out of the corner of my eye. I saw her take something from behind another board nailed low on the studs. She put it down flat on the timber and then saw me watching and said, "Turn around, Cal!"

I looked back at the stacked bales and waited.

"All clear," she said after a little while.

"What were you doing?"

"Never mind."

She started back then, but not on her feet. She inched along, grabbing the edges of the beam and hunching her bottom a little ways forward.

"I can walk over," she said, with a short laugh, "but I can't walk back."

"Just be careful."

She came closer, reaching and hunching, but when she was within a few feet of me—almost close enough to lean and stretch and grab the edge of the platform—she got wobbly and had to stop.

She gripped the edges of the beam and I could see the muscles in her legs. She peeked over the side, immediately straightened and looked at me. I should have done something then, but I was waiting for her to figure it out.

"I think I'm stuck."

"What do you mean?"

"I'm stuck, Cal."

"Just keep doing what you were doing."

"I can't let go to do it!"

"What should I do?"

"I don't know."

I couldn't think of anything. I was scared and my mind wouldn't work. But finally I slid a little forward.

"Better hurry." Julie's eyes were wide, now.

I crawled a little closer to the edge.

"Cal, hurry up!"

I grabbed the edge of the platform, stuck my head out, and pushed until I could hook my elbows over the edge beam. Then I reached as far as I could.

Julie made a grab for me, but our fingers barely touched and she almost fell. She hugged the beam again, hard.

I forced myself forward until I was balanced on my belly. It was terrifying. I thought if I did get ahold of her, we'd both probably fall. But I reached out anyway. I reached as far as I could and said, "Come on!"

This time I got ahold of her fingers. But they were damp, and when she started over sideways they pulled free.

Julie said, "Oh . . . !" and held onto the beam for another instant with just her legs. But it was only for a split second, and then time stopped, and only started again when she landed with a dull thump.

TWENTY

Baxter, Fall, 1966

I don't remember climbing down from the hayloft. Julie was on her side on the floor with her knees bent. Her hair was spread out around her head and her eyes were closed. She was breathing in little hitches. I couldn't think of anything to do but run for Pike. I ran to the side door of the barn and then sprinted for the house.

In the house I yelled, "Help!" and ran upstairs.

Pike came out of the master bedroom. "What are you doing back inside?"

"Julie fell out of the hayloft!"

"What?"

"She's hurt!"

I ran back down.

Pike charged down the stairs and ran through the kitchen ahead of me. When I got to the barn he was kneeling beside Julie.

He looked at me and put his hands on the floor and stood up. "I'm calling the ambulance. Stay here and don't touch her." His voice sounded funny because he was out of breath.

He ran back out of the barn.

I stood next to Julie, my heart squeezed small. She hadn't moved and her eyes were still shut. She was still breathing, at least.

My head was buzzing like hornets.

Pike came back with a blanket, which he draped over Julie. He sat back on his heels and looked at his watch. Then he said, "How did this happen?" His voice was jumpy and strange.

I tried to tell him. When I stopped at the part where Julie got stuck, his eyes narrowed.

"Why didn't you come and get me?"

"I was afraid to leave!"

He didn't say anything more. We just waited together, standing five feet apart, not looking at each other. The whole time I felt like puking.

Finally the ambulance came rushing down the River Road with its lights flashing. It turned up our driveway and stopped. Two men jumped out, grabbed a stretcher from the back, and brought it into the barn. The taller one put a kind hand on my shoulder as he walked past and over to Julie.

My eyes flooded at his touch; everything went blurry

They moved around Julie, knelt, and shined a little pencil-sized flashlight into her eyes, then carefully put a brace around her neck and slowly moved her onto the stretcher.

The tall EMT held her head and neck while the other man eased her legs over. They strapped her in, picked up the stretcher at each end, and carried her out.

"Wait here and tell your mother to meet us at the hospital," Pike said as he walked after them.

They slid Julie into the back of the ambulance, and the taller man took one step up to ride with her while the other walked around to the driver's door.

Pike opened the passenger-side door and got in.

The doors slammed and the flashing lights came on and then the siren. The ambulance rolled down to the end of the driveway, swung into the right lane, and accelerated off toward town.

I watched until the lights were gone, then walked up to the house and sat on the steps. The sun was low over the trees, and it was beginning to cool off.

I looked at the barn, at the apple trees, across the field to the river. It all felt different. I sat there for an hour or so, until my mother showed up.

She came up the driveway in the station wagon, and my heart shrank even more because I was going to have to tell what had happened now, and she would think it was my fault, too.

They stopped and my mother got out one side, and Alvin the other. They slammed their doors and came up the steps. Alvin had his little motor in one hand and a certificate in the other.

He held them out. "Read it and weep!"

"Why are you sitting there?" My mother peered at my face. "What's wrong?"

BURGUNDY CITY

TWENTY-ONE

En Route, 1995

The night before I'm to leave Tampa, I try to get ahold of Rocky Kincaid to see if he can give me a ride into town. But he isn't answering his phone, so I call El Gordo. I didn't want to, because he got pissy when I quit. But I'm not going to hitchhike with two bags to carry and a bus to catch.

I had the phone in the trailer shut off, which means I have to walk down to the corner and use the pay phone. I feed in a quarter and wait for a rush of cars to go by and dial the number.

"Airport Taxi," Fats answers.

"Emile, how's it going?"

He sucks in his breath, and I picture him behind his beat-up desk in a shiny Hawaiian shirt with his face getting blotchy red because he's all worked up.

"I'm a driver short on a goddamn Friday night! How do you think I'm doing?"

"I'm sorry about that."

"Well, get your ass in here and help me out."

"I can't, Fats, I'm sorry."

"Then what the hell are you calling for?"

"I need a ride downtown."

"Jesus," Fats says. "You take the cake, Shaw."

"I don't want a freebie."

"Doesn't matter, we're all stacked up."

"No, I don't need it until tomorrow."

"Why didn't you say so?"

His other line rings, and he puts me on hold. When he comes back he says, "Where you going tomorrow?"

"Greyhound station."

"So you're really leaving?"

"Yeah, just like I told you."

"I thought you were bullshitting."

"Why would I do that?"

"Figured you had a drunk planned and wanted some time off."

"Nope, I'm still on the wagon."

"*Todavía hay milagros!*" His other line rings again, and he says, "Hold on." A minute or two later he comes back and says, "So what time tomorrow?"

"Five-thirty."

"Mother of God." I hear him flip the page of his schedule book over. Then he says, "All right, I'll put you in the book. But you better not no-show on me!"

"I wouldn't."

"I gotta go."

"Hey, Emile."

"What?"

"Aren't you going to wish me luck?"

I can hear his other line ringing again, but he doesn't switch over, and finally he coughs, the way he does when it's either that or show some sort of emotion, and he says, "Listen, *pendejo*, just take care of yourself, okay? Try not to be stupid."

"I'll do my best—" I say, but he's hung up.

It's Neal the Nazi who shows up the next morning, roaring up the aisle between the trailers and skidding to a stop in front of where I'm waiting on the stoop, bags on the grass next to me.

He heaves himself out in all his black-leather-jacketed, tattooed, studded, and bearded glory, walks back to open the trunk, and nods toward the kids' trailer.

"Where's all your little pals?"

"They've moved on."

I heave the duffel I found at Sal's Army in, then stick the cornet case between it and the side of the trunk so it won't bounce around.

"Just like you," Neal says.

"I guess."

He slams the trunk, walks back and falls heavily into his broken-down driver's seat. He smooths his beard down onto his camo shirt, throws the gearshift and yanks us around in a U-turn.

We jounce down to the entrance and run the red light onto Dearborne, and as we start off I take a look back at the trailer park. It always feels strange to move on from a home, even one as shabby as this. Not that I'm all broken up about it, but I have spent part of my life here.

We charge down the road, and I watch the city ahead, all lit up by a burgundy-colored sunrise. We cruise in through the outskirts, ramp up onto the Interstate, and shoot into town. We exit before we get downtown, and at the bottom of a little hill, turn onto the Parkway. Closer to downtown the city is coming awake: people jogging, walking dogs.

"Going back to the boondocks," Neal says.

"Yep."

He blasts his horn at a pedestrian lollygagging across the street in front of us. The guy flips him off, and Neal laughs. "You're in for some culture shock."

"Well, I grew up there."

"Yeah, but you been out in the world."

We turn out of that neighborhood and drive a couple of blocks and he lets me out at the curb in front of the stone-boxy old bus station. He takes my money, drops it into his blue cash bag, and climbs out of the car.

Neal pops the trunk and pulls my gear out, then surprises me by carrying the duffel inside while I take the instrument case. In the terminal he sits the bag down by one of the pew-like benches.

I put my case down and stick out my hand. "Thanks for the lift."

"Y'all take care up there in the sticks."

"I'll do that."

He nods, then about-faces and stalks out.

I wait for him to look back and give me one of his faux salutes, but he just keeps going. So I turn away and step up to the ticket window. I pay for my ride and go back to the bench to wait. There are destination posters on the walls and a couple of homeless guys stretched out on benches with newspapers over their faces.

The bus doesn't leave for a half-hour, and I look at the vending machines lined up against the wall, and think about coffee. But then I imagine how nasty it will likely be, and I stay put.

I hold the cornet case in my lap and wonder what the old farmhouse looks like now. I guess Pike will have kept the property up, being a Realtor and all. My stomach stirs then at the thought that soon I'll be able to see for myself, because I can't really go back to Maine and not stop in there. Even if it means seeing the asshole. And seeing the barn.

I hope I'm ready to see the barn, ready to feel everything that happened that day all over again.

I look down at my instrument case and fight off the urge to take the cornet out. "Blue Summer" is in my head, looking to be heard. But then a heavyset woman comes into the terminal with a young kid who's maybe thirteen, lean and slouchy in jeans and a faded Gators sweatshirt. He gives me a sidelong glance when they walk by, and they go on up to the ticket counter.

I shut my eyes again, listen to the woman talking to the ticket agent. Her voice is low and velvety, and listening to it, I doze off, and don't wake until they call my bus over the intercom.

At the gate, the woman and the boy are waiting. The gate stays closed, and after looking at their backs, I say, "You guys aren't going up to Maine, too, are you?"

The woman turns and smiles. "Lord, no, just to Boston."

When she speaks the kid looks over his shoulder. His eyes slide down to my cornet case.

The woman notices and says, "Georgie here plays the trumpet, too."

"Is that right?"

"Plays in the band back home, don't you, Georgie?"

Georgie says "Yeah," without turning.

"I used to play in my school band, too."

"Was that in Maine?"

"Uh-huh."

"So you're going home?"

"Yeah."

"That's a good thing."

"I guess so."

She squints at me. "Well, Georgie going home is definitely a good thing." She's turned sideways to talk; now she puts a hand on the kid's shoulder and says, "Gramma loves you, Georgie, you know that, but she ain't as young as she used to be."

"Uh-huh," Georgie says.

The bus driver finally shows up: gray uniform, shiny shoes, ticket puncher hanging from his belt. He opens the gate, walks us over to the bus. We're the only ones getting on. He unlocks the baggage compartment and puts my traveling companions' bags inside. Then he shoves my duffel in and without straightening looks at the cornet case at my feet.

"I was hoping I could keep that with me."

He stands up with a grunt, looks at the lady and the boy.

"Well, seeing how we're not that crowded, I guess as long as nobody objects and you don't decide to play reveille at two o'clock in the morning . . ."

"I'll be sound asleep."

"We don't mind," the heavyset lady says.

The driver nods sideways toward the bus's steps.

Georgie and his grandmother board, and I carry the case up after them. It's roomy and dark behind tinted windows. The driver's military-style hat with the shiny brim and big badge sits on his seat. Georgie's grandmother steers him into a seat and works herself in beside him, and I take the one in front of them. I slide my case under the seat in front of me and turn around. "I'm Cal Shaw."

"Loretta McCarty. This is Georgie. We're pleased to meet you, Cal."

She looks at her grandson, and he nods and says "Uh-huh," very softly, and then looks out the window.

Kids fascinate me, especially odd kids, outsider kids—there's a kinship I always feel—and "I wonder what's up with this one."

"Pleased to meet you, too," I say.

"We're going to be riding a long way with Mr. Shaw," Loretta says to the kid, "so we might as well be friends."

"Uh-huh." Georgie looks down at his hands.

"He's just shy." Loretta smiles.

I turn around so Georgie won't have to look at me anymore.

About two minutes later the driver comes aboard, puts his hat on carefully, takes his seat, and levers the door shut. He picks up a clipboard and goes through his checklist. Then he puts the clipboard aside, turns to look over the cabin and finally starts the engine and backs us out of our parking spot. He shifts gears and drives out of the back lot of the bus station and onto the street.

TWENTY-TWO

En Route, 1995

Back in Pinellas County Jail, they had a free-paperback rack at the library, donated by a local church group. I'd started rereading an old, dog-eared copy of *Stranger in a Strange Land* in the pokey, but hadn't finished when I got released, so I took it home with me. And when I was packing I grabbed it to keep me company on the trip to Maine.

Now, reading it on the bus, I see in my mind's eye my father in his recliner with his pipe and the very same book. I see him turning a page reluctantly, like he's sorry to be done with that particular part of the story. I miss him so much it hurts. But I keep reading, and eventually I'm drawn back into Valentine Michael Smith's story, and it keeps me occupied through Orlando and Jacksonville, but then we have a long stretch before our next stop and I fall fast asleep.

I doze right through the rest of Florida and most of Georgia, too. I don't really wake up fully until we cross the river into Savannah. This is early afternoon and it's raining; I can hear it on the roof.

I cock my head this way and that, my neck stiff from leaning against the window, and look at the oil derricks along the riverbanks.

I remember the paperback and pick it up off the floor, find my place, and mark it with a turned-down page. We drive into the low city and go a couple of blocks to the bus station and it's all wet, shiny, gray stone, much bigger than the one in Tampa.

We circle the block and pull into a dock behind the building.

When our driver says "Welcome to Savannah," and opens the door, an older couple who boarded in Orlando walk down the aisle, thank the driver and get off.

The driver turns in his seat to tell us we'll be there for thirty minutes, and can either wait on the bus or go inside. There's a cafeteria inside if we're hungry, but we need to remember that the bus can't wait for anyone who's late coming back.

Then he gets up and follows the older passengers inside.

"Would you mind keeping an eye on Georgie?"

I look at Loretta McCarty and the boy. They've been quiet—maybe dozing, too—and between my book and my dreams, I've sort of forgotten about them.

"I'm going to get us something to eat," Loretta says, "and Georgie, he doesn't like being alone very much, so it would be wonderful if I could leave him here with you."

"I don't mind if he doesn't."

"He won't—will you, Georgie?"

He looks at his hands and shakes his head.

"Can I run in and use the restroom first?"

"Surely."

I double-time it off the bus and find the washroom. I scrub my hands and leave the bathroom and walk around the corner up to the cafeteria, thinking about a burger. But then I decide to save my money and settle for a couple of Snickers bars.

Back on the bus Loretta thanks me again and maneuvers down the aisle.

When she's gone I look around at Georgie. He's sitting with his hands in his lap, staring out the window.

"You doing all right?"

He nods, hunches himself a little closer to the window. I can see uneasiness on his face and in the way he holds himself. There's definitely something going on with him, something that makes him different, and knowing as much as I do about that sort of thing, I feel a bit of kinship.

"She'll be right back, don't worry."

He looks at me, then out the window.

"Want to check out the cornet?"

He looks at me. "Ain't it a trumpet?"

"Nope, cornet."

I pull the case out from under the seat and snap it open. I take the horn from its molded bed and lean over the seat to show it to him.

"Th-that's nice—an Olds."

"What do you play?"

"Conn."

"Student horn?"

He nods, his eyes on the cornet.

"Go ahead."

He's nervous about touching it, but can't resist. I lay it in his hands and he sits back and turns it this way and that. It gleams like gold in the weak light.

"Want to give it a try?"

"In here?"

I take the mouthpiece from its slot in the case and wipe it on my shirt and hand it over.

"I'll keep a lookout."

He looks toward the front of the bus, then sticks the mouthpiece in. He smooshes his lips around to warm them up, then raises the cornet.

He flutters the valves, blows an open B flat, then runs a quiet little minor scale. I can tell right off that he knows what he's doing.

"Very nice."

He looks at me while he keeps playing, still very quietly. There's pride in his eyes because not everyone can play softly. He plays the first couple bars of "America the Beautiful," and I like that he can do it so quietly and still be quite pure. Then he lowers the cornet and says, "That's what we played at the assembly."

"Your first trumpet?"

"Second."

"That doesn't sound right."

"It's 'cause I can't read music."

"You play by ear?"

He nods.

"Chet Baker used to play by ear."

"He did?"

"So they say."

He smiles a little.

"Let me see it a minute."

He hands it over and I wipe off the mouthpiece and open the spit valve and blow a little moisture onto the floor. Then I start into "Blue Summer," trying to be just as quiet and pure as he was. It's still in my head all the time, and I'm glad for a chance to play it in front of someone, but I still haven't figured out exactly how it's supposed to end.

Then Georgie whispers, "Uh-oh."

I turn to see the bus driver coming up the stairwell with a little brown bag in his hand. He glances our way and nods, sits down, and pulls out a wrapped sandwich. He peels the waxed paper away and takes an incongruously dainty bite.

I sneak the cornet back into its case, slide the case under the seat, grin at Georgie.

"Close one."

"Yeah." Softly.

"What he doesn't know won't hurt him."

Georgie swallows a smile.

Loretta comes up the steps then with a shallow cardboard box full of sandwiches. She sidesteps down the aisle and wriggles in beside her grandson.

She gives him a look. "Now what have you been up to?"

"N-n-nothing."

"Don't kid a kidder."

Loretta looks at me. "I think you and Cal might have been up to something."

Georgie lets that sly smile show and Loretta laughs. Then she picks out a sandwich and hands it to him. They're all wrapped in waxed paper like the driver's. She peers at another one end-on, then holds it out to me. "I hope you like chicken salad."

"You got me one?"

"For watching Georgie."

"He didn't really need watching."

Georgie looks at me as he takes another bite.

"All the better." She shakes the sandwich.

"Thank you, then."

"You are so very welcome."

I turn around and wolf my sandwich, and a little later the driver comes down the aisle, holding his clipboard. He checks us off with a nod and keeps walking and checks a couple other passengers off and leans over to punch somebody's ticket.

Then he walks back to his seat, announces over the intercom that we are on our way, next stop, Richmond. He turns the lights down and starts the engine.

When we're moving I look behind me. Loretta smiles. Georgie has withdrawn again and is staring out the window at the lights of the bus station.

I get it completely. For a few minutes he was able to forget himself. But now the cornet's put away and Loretta's back and he has to remember who he is again. That's the way it goes when you feel separate from everybody else. I don't think it matters why. It's just that you can never forget for long, because there's always someone or something around to remind you.

WALKING BOSS

TWENTY-THREE

Baxter, Fall, 1966

Not that forgetting is always a blessing, though. Sometimes it can be anything but, like when I forgot the morning after Julie died. I really did.

Looking back, I know there were reasons. (There were shrinks in the lockup, and one in particular I'd been able to talk to.) I was a kid who'd been traumatized, and who'd only slept for a couple of hours to boot—but in the moment, I didn't understand any of that.

Nobody else had forgotten. They were all in the kitchen—my mother and Alvin at the table, Pike leaning on the counter—and when I walked in, soft-whistling a piece I'd been studying for Uncle Gus, they all stared at me in disbelief.

Then it hit me and I remembered everything.

First I remembered fighting with Pike, and then I remembered Julie falling and the hospital, and that was all I could think about. It was as if she had died all over again.

I saw her suddenly arching her back in the hospital bed, opening her eyes wide, and falling back. I heard an alarm begin to ring. Nurses and doctors came running, and we had to leave while they tried to save her, and I prayed the whole time we were in the waiting room by the nurses' station.

But there was no miracle, and when the doctor joined us a few minutes later we could see it in his face; he didn't have to say a word.

But he said "I'm so terribly sorry" anyway, and then led us back to Julie's room and held the door so we could walk past him and say good-bye.

Pike stood aside while we went to Julie in her bed.

Alvin took her hand, and I brushed the hair off her forehead. She wasn't cold, but seemed small and lonely with the blankets and those starchy hospital sheets bunched around her.

My mother took her hand and knelt beside the bed.

I don't know how long we were with her. But eventually the doctor came back and spoke to Pike, who nodded and took our mother by the shoulders and eased her away from the bed. Then he looked at Alvin and me and said, "We have to go."

We followed them out of the room and down the corridor, past nurses who knew what had happened, but not how to speak to us about it, and we walked outside and found our car, and we waited while Pike went back to make arrangements. Then he returned and drove us away through the dark. It was a clear night, with thousands of stars low and bright in the sky, and it was silent in the car all the way back.

I remembered all that in a flash, and then, in the kitchen that morning after, I looked at my mother and said, "Oh no, Mum, I forgot. I'm sorry!"

She put a hand over her mouth, jumped up and ran to the door. Alvin and Pike followed her outside, and I stood there, hating myself for being such an idiot. Then I went out onto the porch too.

"I'm sorry!" I said again, and my voice cracked.

My mother said, "I know you are, Calvin," and rocked her chair forward to put an arm around me. But when I tried to throw my arms around her, so that she could hold me closer, she caught them and held me off.

"I'm sorry," she said. "I can't."

I backed away and stuck my hands in my pockets. It felt like they all wanted me to leave, so I walked down the steps and across the lawn to the field. I moved slow, hoping my mother might call me back, but she didn't, and I walked all the way down to the apple trees by the river.

I found out later that Pike made the most of my absence by planting his own version of the tragedy in my family's heads. According to him, I could have helped her in the hayloft, but I'd been too scared and had frozen; had even been unable to run and get him, until it was too late. He didn't want to actually blame me, because I was just a kid, but it all could have turned out very differently if I'd fetched him in time. He might have talked her down from that beam, or even caught her when she fell.

It was a calculated attempt to make sure all of the guilt and blame belonged to me. And it worked, because there was no one to tell my side of the story, and because I'd already been guilty of forgetting.

It worked also because Pike, my mother, and Alvin *needed* it to work. Pike, for obvious reasons, and the other two, because they'd stood by while he'd bullied Julie and now she was gone and that would never change.

And there was one final reason why it worked. I never tried very hard to defend myself. I couldn't, because I agreed. In my heart I knew that I'd failed Julie. I still do, even now. I can hate Pike for what he did, but there will always be a broken part of me that believes he was right—that Julie died because of me.

That night, when Alvin looked down at me from the upper bunk and said, "Why did you have to chicken out, Cal?" in a choked voice, I couldn't think of a single thing to say back.

TWENTY-FOUR

Baxter, Fall, 1966

So I was cast adrift all over again, a little more than two years after my father had died. Only it was even worse this time, because there was no Julie to help me get by. It really wasn't easy to be that kid. Nobody liked me anymore, and nothing I did seemed to make any difference. I tried more apologies, but they didn't help. "Cal," my mother finally said, "I'm sorry, but I can't keep talking about your sister."

Then I tried *showing* I was sorry. You remember the movie *Cool Hand Luke*—how they punished Lucas Jackson by making him dig a ditch and then fill it back in, over and over, until he couldn't take it anymore? Remember how afterward he trotted around in his ankle chains, doing everything the Walking Boss wanted, like his broken little pet?

Well, I was pretty much like Lucas Jackson with my mother for a while. But it was all wasted effort. Eventually she said, "Cal, stop hovering!" and then I didn't know what to do with myself.

I missed my sister with a stone-cold ache, and I felt like a stranger in my own home. One day I couldn't stand it anymore and just walked out of the house and took off along the riverbank. I was pretty sure no one would care that I was gone, or how long I stayed away.

I hiked all the way up to the Old Settlers Cemetery and sat down next to one of the ancient stone markers and I just gave up. I let it all flood out—all the shapes and shades that had been prying at corners and testing gates since I'd gotten up that morning. I groaned and wailed until my stomach hurt, and when it finally let up and the old Mean Troubles had slunk away (not far; I could still feel them nearby, like coyotes around a campfire), it made me feel a little better. Not for any good reason, but in practical terms. See, I'd still had this tiny hope that my mother would like me again somehow, and losing that had been the price of their departure. When they took that last bit of hope with them, it freed me up to finally see a way forward.

Sitting against the old slab, drained now and clearheaded, I decided that I would be stoic, like the tragic and noble heroes in my dad's mythology books. I would accept my fate as the outcast because I deserved it, and while accepting it wouldn't make me happy, maybe I wouldn't have to be Luke Jackson anymore either.

I thought this through a couple of times, sniffling and sighing. Then I got to my feet, wiped my eyes on my sleeve, spat on the ground by the grave marker, squared my shoulders, and started walking back to the house.

When I got there I went silently past my mother sitting in her rocker with a magazine and a cigarette, and when she looked up I met her eyes just long enough to let her know silently that I wouldn't be bothering her anymore.

I looked in the living room and saw Alvin with his eyes glued to the TV. He didn't even notice me, so I decided to skip the meaningful look I'd prepared for him.

I went straight up to my bedroom. On my bunk I stared out the window at the field.

"That's that," I said, and it felt correct to have decided to be tragic and noble, to move on from any sort of misguided hope that my family would ever love me again.

Afterwards I would join them for meals, but not much else, and I went for longer and longer walks in the woods, and bike rides. I would walk down to the river and sit under an apple tree and watch the water go by. I spent a lot of time in the barn. That part of it was useful, at least.

Music was the one thing I couldn't *not* care about, and I'd take my horn to the barn to practice. I began to learn a lot faster, because I was more serious. Over the next few months I discovered that if you played with everything you had, it could become a conversation, or an exclamation, or a lament.

Sometimes that could get a little dangerous.

I'd be playing something slow, in a minor key, and it would hit me. I'd put the horn down and look up at the hayloft, and I'd think about Julie, and sometimes I'd wonder about taking that walk myself. Because I might fall, and that would be the perfect ending, right? They'd have no choice but to forgive me.

But I never quite had the gumption to try it.

So I settled for staying on my separate path.

I suppose in the back of my mind I still wondered if my mother would notice how distant I'd become and would care enough to do something about it, but that never happened, and after a while I let even that wisp of a hope go and it all began to seem normal. I got used to it, I guess. It was less trouble, and there was a certain sense of relief.

Everybody else seemed fine with it, too.

Mostly they left me alone. Pike even laid off about chores. He'd won. I wasn't important enough to bother with any more. And as time went by things got pretty well fixed, with me as more of a boarder than a family member.

It was another distinct stretch of my youth.

I got a little older and still felt sad sometimes, but for the most part, it was better this way.

And there was always Uncle Gus.

He'd been demoted by Pike from *family friend* to *just the music teacher*, but still knew most of what was going on and understood that I was getting a raw deal. And maybe he didn't have it in him to confront a guy like Pike, but he helped in his own way by making clear I was welcome to come over anytime I wanted.

With all my barn playing I got good enough that he'd let me use his Committee—a huge privilege—while he grabbed the alto, which meant we were going to play together, which also meant that we would be trading off solos.

He wasn't as proficient on the sax, so I could keep up, and when we were trading and I hit something cool, he would point at me and grin, and I would have one of those forgetful moments where I felt happy for a little while.

So I was a lodger at home, a musician at Uncle Gus's and a little of both everywhere else.

At school I was stuck mostly by myself, because the kids I'd grown up with had pretty much written me off. A kid's world can be cruel, and sometimes it doesn't take much. I'd changed after losing my father, and that had started it: The other kids gave me a certain amount of sympathy, but then, being kids, moved on.

Maybe they'd have come back once I was myself again, but Pike showed up before that could happen, and then Julie fell out of the hayloft, and when the story went around that I might have saved her if I hadn't been a weakling and a coward (thanks, Alvin), my odds of bouncing back took a pretty serious hit. (And of course, it didn't help that I mostly agreed.)

Even when new kids moved to town, nothing changed. Someone would always fill them in, and they would be only too happy to join the rest of the pack—still including my brother—in leaving me to fend for myself.

On a couple of occasions a new boy would decide to take it a little further and pick on me, to grease his own skids. I'd always been fairly scrappy, and even as guilt-ridden as I was, would only take so much before pushing back, which led to fights, which made things worse, because the school authorities figured since I was the common denominator, I must be the problem.

Which of course I found unfair.

Which made my attitude and behavior worse.

So on it went, and after a while I became fixed into an odd sort of position: decent student (I couldn't help it), talented musician (my trumpet was everything), and at the same time, surly loner who often seemed *mad at the world* (as my principal put it during one of his one-on-one lectures).

Sometimes people tried to see past that facade.

When I got to high school, Mr. Wilkins, the senior janitor, spotted me right off as needing a friend, and would wink and say, "How we doing today, kid?" when we passed in the corridors. And our band director, Mr. Booker, treated me well enough, which encouraged the other kids in the band to give me a certain amount of respect, too—at least while we were together.

But otherwise, I'd have to say the tide was definitely against me.

Baxter, 1970

A tide can work in different ways, though, and while this one may have carried me away from the popular crowd, it also eddied me into places where the other marginal kids tended to wash up: the dead end of the corridor by the boys' room, the unofficial smoking zone in the birch grove behind the school, the All-Purpose Room (which was dark and empty between assemblies and gym classes). By the time I was a sophomore that actually gave me a niche—a few of us began slouching around together—and made the next couple of years a little more bearable, an interlude of sorts.

There never was a time when I got over Julie's death or my failure to save her: It could hit me like a thunderclap at a moment's notice. But just having cronies meant there would be moments of distraction and even pleasure, like a spirited four-bar riff where you let it all hang out, even knowing that you'll have to bring it back to the melody.

There were two guys I regularly hung out with: Chuck Lamar—a rugged boy who lived on Depot Street, down by the train tracks; and Bobby Berube, a snarly near-midget who lived with his mother, two houses down from Chuck. They were *poor kids* I'd known since first grade who were now wannabe hoods. They wore trucker jackets with the collars turned up and combed their dark hair back into greasy pompadours.

We were wary with each other at first, but as time went on, we got friendlier, and then one day in the cafeteria it all came together.

Chuck, who'd been carefully tending his DA with a comb, said, "Look at the cool kids watching." And after Bobby and I turned to look (at a table of smiling jocks and cheerleaders), he said, "They think we're all shitheads."

After which we began calling ourselves the Shitheads.

Naming ourselves was another kind of giving up, but a cheeky one. And like my earlier noble/tragic persona, it gave me some respite from the gloom. There's strength even in small numbers, and now we got bolder, grinning insolently back at the cool kids, Chuck even trading punches with one of them in study hall after the teacher had stepped out. (The guy quit after taking one square in the nose, which we considered a great victory, and which elevated Chuck to Walking Boss.)

We were Baxter High's first attempted gang. After school, unless I had band, we'd walk to the pool hall uptown, careful not to piss off the *actual* hoods there: lean and sallow guys who worked at the shoe shop in Emery Falls, two miles upriver, who carried their cigarettes in turned-up T-shirt sleeves, and who would buy us beer, but only on impulse, nothing to depend on.

Or sometimes we'd gather at the iron bridge over the Baxter. There was a space under one end of the bridge, formed by girders and concrete braces that had been added to the original granite footings. We would muster there—cars thumping across above us—to smoke and cuss, and when we snapped our cigarette butts into the water they would hiss like three-dimensional exclamation points.

Mainly it was the three of us, but other boys would come and go, and sometimes the odd girl who was working her way toward not giving a damn. Becky O'Dell even joined us in my sophomore year, after she'd lost her place with the cool kids. Over the years it had become important that she lived in a double-wide, that her father was a second-rate lobsterman, and that she was mysteriously knock-kneed and not lithe cheerleader material.

The capper was when she came down with a case of mononucleosis that cost her most of a school year and put her back in my class; after that we began to bump into each other more, and started exchanging smiles. No doubt she was lonely, too, because one day she came hobbling up in the cafeteria and said, "So what are you little kids up to?"

She ate with us after that, and joined us when we skipped study hall to hang out behind the stage curtain in the All-Purpose Room, and behind the school when we snuck out during lunch to have a smoke.

"You smoke?" I said, looking over Bobby's head at her—he was grimly sucking the life out of one himself—and she tapped the pack against her palm, pulled a skinny cig out with her lips, and said "Sure do" out of one side of her mouth.

"How long's that been going on?"

"Since I started working on the boat."

"Your father lets it go?"

"What's he gonna say? They all smoke, too."

She joined us under the bridge, on afternoons when the wind was howling and she didn't have to haul. (When I asked how she'd discovered our hideouts, she said everybody knew about our little juvenile delinquent gatherings.)

I wasn't entirely sure how I felt about Becky coming on board. She triggered lots of Julie feelings, of course, and she'd never tried to close the distance that had opened between me and my childhood friends. But the Julie stuff wasn't her fault, and she'd never been mean to me; plus, she was as natural and likable as ever.

So I kept my doubts to myself, and then one day she saved us from Chief Foss, head of the Baxter PD, and how could I have doubts after that?

I WOULDN'T BE
AT ALL SURPRISED

TWENTY-SIX

Baxter, 1970

We'd gathered at the old stone pier down past the Old Settlers Cemetery, because Chuck had heisted some Black Label beer from his parents and we didn't want to drink it at the bridge; that was too close to town, and Chief Foss liked to roust us from there when he was in a fractious mood.

That afternoon Chuck passed a note in study hall for us to meet after supper. (Passing notes cut across social lines; even the cool kids would honor a note.)

Getting out of our homes wasn't any trouble.

Chuck and Bobby's parents didn't care what they were up to, and I pretty much came and went as I liked, as long as I didn't do anything to call attention to myself. (Things had worsened between Pike and me recently, but I was still trying to make it to graduation.)

So after supper that night I just said "Going out—see you later" to my mother, grabbed my jacket and left. I rode my Schwinn down the River Road and hid it in a tall culvert that took a little stream under the pavement.

Chuck's and Bobby's bikes were already there, tires in the dirty water, leaning against the corrugated wall. I left my bike and walked the rest of the way, then ran through the graveyard and the pine groves to the river.

It was low tide, and dark mudflats spread out from the old stone pier to the pinched flow of the water. The sun was behind the trees, and it was shadowy and mysterious.

They were sitting on one of the granite slabs that made up the pier, and hadn't started in on the beer yet. It made me happy that they'd waited.

"About time, asshole," Chuck said.

I took a beer from him. He handed Bobby one, too, and we all popped the tops—that wicked hiss—and leaned forward to click the cans together.

"Drink, Shitheads," Chuck said.

We lit cigarettes and nursed the beers. It was piss-warm, but that was all right. I hadn't really developed a taste for the stuff, but I could get it down, cold or warm, because of how it made me feel. (After a whole sixteen-ouncer I'd get a glow and my mind would settle amazingly. I thought it was something, that beer could do that.)

We sipped from our cans.

"Did you catch Dana Knight's dress?" Bobby said.

Chuck raised his beer to toast Dana's mini-dress, which I'd gotten a better look at than the rest of them. I was still in the Academic section, like her, and I'd gone up to sharpen my pencil in English class so I could check her out. (I was sixteen now, and sex was everything to me, even though I knew nothing about it.)

The sun dropped lower and it was getting dark by the river, and we sprawled on the warm granite slabs, enjoying our little buzz, and complained about school, and argued Beatles versus Stones. We talked about the Red Sox and whether Tony C. would ever make a comeback, and then Chuck lifted his T-shirt and showed us the purple and yellow bruise where his old man had slugged him.

It made me wince. "What'd he hit you for?"

"Smart-mouthing. I called him a drunk."

"He is a drunk," Bobby said.

"Yeah, but he don't like it when you call him one."

"That stinks."

"Yeah, but what can you do?"

Chuck was telling us about his plan to get his parents to sign off on joining the marines next year, after he turned seventeen ("They'll be glad to get rid of me"), when we heard an outboard boat chugging up the river.

In case it was the Clam Cops we stomped the empty cans flat and slid them into cracks between the granite slabs. Then we hid behind the pier until the boat should pass.

But it didn't motor past. It swung in close given the low tide and throttled back, and then Becky's raspy voice came to us across the flats. You could always tell her voice.

"Ahoy, Cal!"

"Ahoy!" I yelled back.

"Hey listen, Foss is onto you guys!"

"What's that?"

"Foss is coming! I came to get you out of here."

We heard a car driving down the road then, and the hair stood up on my neck. But it went right on by. Only seconds later, though, another car came along, and we all held our breath to listen. I could hear the car coming and the water splashing lightly against Becky's boat. The car turned into the little gravel parking lot by the cemetery.

"Holy shit!" Chuck said.

"Hurry up!" Becky yelled.

We yanked our shoes and socks off, rolled up our pant legs, and went slopping through the mud, hoping we wouldn't step into a honeypot and disappear.

Becky held the boat steady while we splashed through the thigh-deep water and crawled over the side, rocking the little boat, and as we were still getting settled she turned to run carefully out into the channel.

She wagged a thumb, upstream or down-, and when I pointed toward town, she fed it some gas and the bow went up a couple of inches and we plowed ahead, overloaded and low in the water.

It was dark enough now that the water was silvery. Back toward the pier we could see flashlights moving through the trees. I looked at Chuck and we laughed.

I turned back to Becky. Her chestnut mop—dark in the weak light—was snapping around and she had a big grin. She was wearing jeans and a fisherman's sweater and you couldn't tell she had bum legs; with her hand on the throttle she looked wild and pretty, and my mind shifted suddenly to see her that way.

"How'd you know?" I yelled above the engine noise.

"I heard my old man on the VHF!" (Her father was a reserve police officer, and apparently Foss had called his boat in to be part of the posse.)

"How'd they find out?"

"Somebody peeked at the note and squealed."

Becky had waited until her father left for the police station, then told her mother she was going fishing and ran down to their dock and shoved off in the outboard. She knew the river, so it was no problem running up in the twilight. In fact, she'd thought it a pretty cool adventure.

I told her we'd hidden our bikes in the culvert, and when we got up to where the little offshoot cut through the flats, she swung us in until the boat scraped softly on the mud.

We stood in the shallow water. I had my shoes and socks under one arm. I said, "Becky to the rescue!"

"Don't ask me why."

"Thanks, Beck!" the other guys said.

"Let me go so I can get home before he does!"

We shoved her off and she throttled up and raced off downriver. Her father had a fifteen-horse on that boat, and it moved along pretty well.

We splashed through the shallows and slopped over the mudflats to the riverbank, wiping our muddy feet with handfuls of marsh grass, putting on our socks and sneakers.

We rolled the bikes out of the culvert and headed home, my friends toward town, and me, the other way. I chortled all the way back at our narrow escape, but stopped when I rode up the driveway and saw Pike waiting on the porch. It was still pretty early, so it wasn't that.

I swung off the bike and let it down on the grass.

Pike had put on some belly weight and looked more than ever like a bear. And like a bear, he still looked capable of moving his mass fast enough to hurt you.

That was a concern, because I'd felt that old meanness trying to resurface in him lately. I thought it was tied to me becoming a Shithead and the attitude change. I still tried to keep a low profile, but it hadn't been as easy lately, and Pike's antennae were up in case he might have to make sure I didn't somehow gain a little confidence in some way.

"Where you been?" he said as I walked up.

I stuck my fingers in my jeans pockets, shrugged with my elbows. "Nowhere special."

He looked down at me from the top step.

"Well, we had a little visit from Chief Foss."

Foss and Pike were pals who went shooting rats together at the sand pit; I should have figured they'd talk.

"Is that right?"

"Yeah. Seems they had a report about some kids drinking down by the river. He was wondering if you might be one of them. I told him I wouldn't be at all surprised."

"Had my back, huh?"

This was sassier than usual, and I could see the surprise in his little porcine eyes. I guess I was surprised, too. But I was still fired up after escaping from Foss and his posse.

Pike came down the steps. "You smell like a brewery."

I elbow-shrugged again and didn't say anything.

He came up close. We were the same height now, and I didn't think he liked that I could look him in the eye.

"So who were you out with?"

"Nobody."

"Lord, I hate a liar." He reached out and gave me a two-fingered poke in the chest. "That Lamar kid, huh? That Berube, right? Those greasy little punks."

He jabbed me again, hard enough to knock me off balance. I caught a whiff of alcohol from him, then.

"Keep your hands to yourself," I said.

"What's that?" Jab.

"I said, keep your hands off me."

My chest was starting to hurt, and it was pissing me off. When
he tried it again I knocked his arm away.

He grinned and held two fingers out, tauntingly.

I thought he'd had a few, had decided it was time to let me know
who was boss again, and I'd just given him the perfect opportunity.
Normally I would have backed down at this point; I would have
thought about how little time I had left at this house.

But I'd had a couple of beers, and I was fresh off an adventure
with the boys, and I'd listened to Chuck talk about not taking any
shit from his old man. So when he tried another two-fingered poke,
I pushed him in the chest, hard, with both hands.

"Leave me the hell alone!"

He lost *his* balance, and stopped grinning. His piggy eyes narrowed,
and I wanted so much to step up and punch him in the face. But Pike
still outweighed me by a hundred pounds, so I hesitated.

He lunged and got me in a headlock. I wrestled with him, tried
pushing his arms away, but I was helpless. He walked me around in a
circle, squeezing until I couldn't breathe, muttering things like "You
think you're a tough guy, huh?" and finally I stopped trying to get
free and let myself go slack.

He held on a little longer—my head grossly tight against his damp
armpit—and then slung me down onto the gravel.

I sat up, coughed and hacked. He was breathing hard and his shirt
was untucked. I got a knee underneath and stood up.

He pointed at me and said "Consider yourself grounded." Then
he walked back to the porch, still panting, tucking his shirttail in, his
fish-belly-white skin showing and then disappearing.

He went into the house and a minute later came back outside
with my mother.

I was standing with my bike, shaken, contemplating riding up to Uncle Gus's.

"There he is," Pike said. "Our very own delinquent."

I let the bike back down.

"Calvin? Is it true?"

"Why ask me?"

"I want you to tell me."

"You always believe him anyway."

"Watch your mouth." Pike looked at my mother. "So he's grounded."

"Oh, Calvin," my mother said.

"For a month." Pike stood up straight like a drill sergeant. "We clear? And that includes your so-called uncle."

"What's he got to do with anything?"

"Grounded means grounded."

"Should we really take away his music, Randy?"

"He doesn't give a damn about anything else." He put his hands on his hips. "A month. And if I hear you're still sneaking around, we'll talk some more."

He hocked and spat over the porch railing, then turned and went hulking back into the house, stepping sideways past my mother in the doorway.

"Nice guy you got there," I said.

"You're underage," my mother said, and went inside.

I looked at my bike and thought about riding to Gus's. But I knew Pike would come after me, and Uncle Gus would back down. I thought about running away. But back then they just caught you and took you home or put you in reform school. Nobody thought about taking you away from your parents, especially if your stepfather was a big shot and best buddies with the chief of police.

So I was stuck.

I picked up a rock from the driveway and threw it as hard as I could. It hit the grass and bounced into the barn a foot from the side door.

When he heard the bang Pike opened the kitchen door and we looked at each other. Then he smiled and shut the door.

TWENTY-SEVEN

Baxter, 1970

I served my sentence and did my best to not trigger Pike at home, but I wasn't going to stop seeing my friends, especially now that they included Becky O'Dell.

See, after the river rescue, I was a goner.

I didn't care about her legs, or that she was a year older, or even about the rumors that she'd slept around a bit when she'd been in with the In-Crowd.

None of that mattered, because I'd seen her perched on the aft seat of her father's boat as she snatched us away from certain doom, like some pretty Dunkirk hero, and just like that, I was madly in love.

Not that I knew what the hell to do about it.

I'd never been any kind of Don Juan even before I was a Shithead. So it was Becky who had to get things moving, which she did on our gang's last under-the-bridge meeting before summer vacation.

It was cool under the bridge, and we'd been there a couple of hours. Then Chuck decided he'd go and see the man recruiting blueberry rakers, who was holding a sign-up session that day on the town hall lawn.

Bobby Berube thought he might give it a try, too.

Chuck looked at me, and I said, "Nah, I don't think so."

Raking blueberries was a good way to make money, but I'd been dying for a chance to be alone with Becky.

"Suit yourself."

Chuck and Bobby levered themselves up and out of our alcove, sneakered feet levitating last. We listened to them run along the footbridge, and then I lit a cigarette and offered it to Becky, rumpling the empty pack so she'd notice I was giving her my last one.

"No, thanks."

She was sitting cross-legged, wearing jeans and a boy's white T-shirt. She'd gotten pretty curvy. I swallowed and looked at the water. It had a greenish cast out where the sun hit it, but was a cool, thin blue under the shadow of the bridge. I threw the crumpled cigarette pack into the water, turned my head and caught her looking at me.

"How's things at home?" she said.

"Peachy keen."

She laughed.

"Two more years." I watched the water splash against the cement pilings.

"Are you going to make it?"

"I hope so."

She moved and I looked over. She was rocking up on one hip so she could straighten her legs and hang them over the side. Then her feet were inches above the running water, and her hands flat on the concrete, and she put her cheek against her raised shoulder and looked back at me.

When I only swallowed and sat there, she laughed again under her breath. I was afraid then that she'd be disappointed in me, and managed to blurt out, "Becky . . . !"

"Yeah?"

My face felt hot. "Shit. I don't know."

"Well, if you don't, I don't either."

I gritted my teeth. "Becky . . ."

"You already said that."

I hung my head, shook it back and forth.

"You're something else, Shaw."

"Hell," I said. "Damn it."

"Don't worry about it. You're just a kid."

"I'm not that much of a kid."

"Yeah, you are." She crossed one leg over the other and leaned toward me against her stiff arm.

"I just . . ."

"Shut up."

She hunched herself sideways until we were shoulder to shoulder. It was a challenge, and I was just brave enough to put an arm around her. After which she put a hand on my chest and looked into my eyes.

Oh, my heart went soaring. A car thumped by above, which made us feel even more secluded, and then she lifted her lips to mine. We kissed, and I looked at her and she grinned. I fell a long way into her eyes. Our lips came together again, and when we stopped I could feel her heart beating.

"Egad," I said.

"You're pathetic," she said, and pulled me close again.

TWENTY-EIGHT

Baxter, 1970

After that Becky and I were a duo, together whenever she wasn't helping her father, and I wasn't studying with Uncle Gus or mowing lawns with Bobby Berube (who'd failed at blueberry raking because, he claimed, his arms were too short).

We couldn't hang out at my house even if Pike wasn't around, because he was always liable to show up and be an asshole. And I told you about her father. So we'd meet on the River Road and walk through the woods to the stone pier, and we would sit on the grass near the remains of an old homestead (relics of a stone foundation) and watch the water drift along.

We'd smoke cigarettes and drink beer if we'd managed to cop some, and we'd talk about everything. We even talked about Julie. I'd never talked to anybody about Julie before, but I told her about the fight with Pike and the truth about how I'd tried to grab her on the beam.

"I could have saved her."

"You were a little boy."

She would hold me until I felt better, and after a little we'd kiss, and the gentle kisses would gradually turn into make-out sessions that got us both all worked up, and then I would try to grab something I shouldn't and Becky would pull away.

"I'm sorry," she'd say.

"It's all right."

It *was* all right with me at first; I was thrilled just to have a girlfriend.

But as I got more comfortable I couldn't help but feel disappointed. I saw her as experienced, after all; she could teach me.

Sometimes I even got cranky. And one day when I did she decided she should try to explain. She'd said, "No, Cal!" and I'd taken my fingertips out of the waistband of her panties, had slid away from her on the sand and had lit up a Lucky Strike. I wasn't saying anything and I wouldn't look at her.

"Try not to take it personally, okay?"

"Okay." I blew smoke at the river.

"It's just that with you I want things to be different."

"From what?"

"From the way it's been sometimes."

I took another drag, looked out at the water. A heron lifted up from the marsh grass fifty yards away and flew slowly away from us, looking prehistoric. I thought about Alvin and dinosaurs. Then I let the smoke out and said, "We could try it and see." I looked back at her then and we smiled.

"We can't," Becky said. "Because you can't just let a boy do what he wants. I learned that the hard way. Because then that boy will like you less. You'd think it would work the opposite, but it doesn't." She shook her head. "And I don't want you to like me less."

"I never would," I said, but I wondered, because I'd heard guys talk about their supposed conquests, and none of them had seemed the least bit concerned about jumping from one girl to another.

"It's not that I don't believe you, Cal."

"Then what's the problem?"

"I've believed boys before."

I watched the heron disappear around a bend in the river, flying below the tree line. Then I took a last drag on the Lucky and snapped it away.

"All right," I said, and I meant it, too. Maybe I was desperate to make actual love (I was sure it would be more than the rutting guys bragged about), but I was also grateful just to be able to hold her, to kiss her, and sometimes—when she got *really* worked up—even touch her breasts.

The important thing was that she'd busted into my loneliness in a way that the Shitheads never could. I knew she was thinking about me when we were apart. I knew I could tell her anything without fear. One afternoon at Memorial Park in Baxter I even told her about the scary shapes and colors that sometimes invaded my mind, that I'd never mentioned to anyone else.

"That sounds horrible," she'd said.

"Oh, you get used to it."

"Where do they come from?"

I told her about falling out of the tree, and how after the headaches had finally gone away the other stuff had started showing up.

"You're a strange one, Shaw," she said, and put her arms around me on the park bench.

Sometimes if Becky didn't have to go fishing, she would meet me at Uncle Gus's. After my wrestling match with Pike in the driveway, I'd been spending time at his house, sometimes even sleeping over. Pike was just as glad to be rid of me, but I was careful not to overdo it, because I didn't want to impose—Uncle Gus had his solitary routines—and because I was afraid Pike would think I was getting away with something.

Uncle Gus had always liked Becky, though. As far as he was concerned she was welcome anytime. If he had a student we'd hang out upstairs and play cribbage on the board he and my father had nearly worn out during their days in the navy. And we'd put on his Blue Note and Riverside records.

Becky had never listened to that kind of music—they only played country-and-western on the boat—but she was willing to give it a chance, except for the more radical stuff, and after a while even mused about joining the school band. ("Maybe I could play the triangle!")

But her father vetoed that idea: too time-consuming.

Anyway, we were together, and I was thrilled, and it really didn't matter that we weren't doing everything that she might have done with some of the In Crowd Boys.

Until school started again in the fall, that is, when suddenly, it did.

TWENTY-NINE

Baxter, 1971–1972

Things can change fast in high school, and it was different for me that next year. I had a girlfriend, along with my pals; I was taller, and had somehow added a few muscles. The other difference was that I got a little full of myself. (Yeah, sometimes it doesn't take long.)

Other girls would say "Hi," now, and smile at me. It was as if I'd crossed some threshold over the summer. One of these girls played clarinet in the band. Her name was Donna York, and she'd been part of the In-Crowd at one time, but had become a free agent after several family vacations in San Francisco, where she'd discovered the counterculture.

She and her two best friends wore shapeless dresses and carried books by Ferlinghetti and Kerouac. They flashed the peace sign instead of waving see-you-later, and that fall gave each other Age of Aquarius nicknames like "Rain" and "Peace."

Donna called herself "Dharma." She was tall and confident and wore headbands over her long sandy-blonde hair. She went braless when she could get away with it, and was supposed to be a free-love hippie.

She was also a good musician, and when Mr. Booker asked her to join our band's jazz combo, we were together after school three days a week. Before long I was wondering what it would be like to kiss her.

We'd make eye contact during band sessions, and sometimes leaving practice she'd bump me with her hip at something I might have said, and then things took a big leap during a band trip to the state capital to compete for a chance to go to DC, for the Cherry Blossom Festival.

Halfway to Augusta, Dharma left her seat with Peace and Rain, walked down the aisle, and asked me where Becky O'Dell had been that day in school.

And when I told her Becky had stayed home with the flu, she took my hand, held it between her uniform-bound breasts, and said, "Poor Cal—you were alone all day!"

We sat together the rest of the trip, and after the competition (second place, but I won First Trumpet), we walked back to the bus together and took the same seat for the ride home. I knew I was doing wrong, but couldn't help myself.

On the way back Dharma leaned against me while we talked, and looked up at me with her sleepy eyes. After the sun went down and it was dim enough inside the bus, I kissed her. It felt terrible to do, but I loved it. She kissed differently than Becky, more aggressively, which made it a whole new thrilling thing.

We weren't the only ones paired off, and when all the heavy breathing got noticeable, Mr. Booker had the driver snap the inside lights on. Then he said, "Hands where I can see 'em!", and we all raised our hands. But then Mr. Booker laughed and had the lights turned off again.

I could barely walk by the time we pulled into the lot at Baxter High, because over the last mile or two I'd slipped my hand between the brass buttons of her double-breasted uniform and she'd put her hand on my leg and squeezed.

"See you around?" Dharma said when we got off the bus, and then she and her friends walked off, heads together, chattering, looking back at me.

I rode my bike to school the next day instead of taking the bus with Becky. I was afraid my face or manner would give something away. But when I saw Becky between classes, I could tell she already knew something had happened. There'd been too many witnesses for someone not to have said something.

She'd caught me at my locker, had given me a hard look, and said, "So how was the band trip, Cal?"

"It was all right." I felt like a traitor.

"Better than all right, from what I heard."

So I confessed that I'd sat with Donna York, and we'd flirted during the bus ride. But I swore it was only because I was lonely without her, and told her I loved her and that it wouldn't happen again.

Becky went off to her next class, and took another two after that to decide she'd give me another chance. We spent lunch period together outside by the birch grove behind the school. She was still standoffish for a while, but eventually when I kissed her, it felt right, like we were already halfway back to normal. When the bell rang I held her close and said I was sorry and told her I loved her. I swore to myself that I wouldn't screw up again. I wouldn't be weak, and I would do my best to avoid Donna York.

But I still saw her after school, for combo practice. And she could talk jazz, and had those sleepy eyes and that feline confidence, and there'd been all that promise in her touch on the bus, and I couldn't help being friendly with her.

One day after practice she couldn't get her clarinet apart.

"Cal, could you help me?" Dharma said, and I snapped my own case shut and went over to take a look. It came apart easily, and she laughed and said, "I guess I wasn't doing it right!" She put it away and we walked together out of the All-Purpose Room and down the corridor to the front door.

Outside I started right off for the bike rack, but Dharma's ride wasn't there yet, and she said, "Aren't you going to keep me company?"

"I should get going."

"Wait a little while, at least. Please?"

So I walked back to wait with her.

"Let's go sit on the bench."

We sat on the bench next to the flagpole, and pretty soon were the only kids left. All the staff had gone home, too, except for the janitors, and we were pretty much alone. The sun was shining over the brick school onto the bench, and us.

Dharma clasped her hands together and stretched her arms out. "Isn't this nice?" She leaned against me and smiled. And then she lifted her chin and kissed me. I'd known since walking back from the bike rack that I'd let her do it. I kissed her back, and with that, everything that had started on the bus trip was rekindled.

When the kiss ended, she looked at me and let her hand rest on my thigh. I could feel myself nudging her hand, and then she let her hand nudge back, and I nearly passed out.

When her mother showed up, Dharma brought me over to the car—a red MG—and introduced me.

"Cal's in the jazz ensemble, Mother."

"Wonderful! Cal, you'll have to come to dinner!"

"Sure," I said, and then Donna kissed me on the lips—her mother only smiled—and walked around to the passenger side. She looked amusedly at me before getting in.

After they drove off I strapped my trumpet case onto the bike carrier and pedaled home. I was ashamed and excited, and wondered if I could put this behind me as another slipup, and then I wondered what would happen next.

What happened next was that Dharma got bolder.

I'd be walking with Becky, and we'd pass Dharma in the hallway and she'd give me an open look. Sometimes she'd even sashay up and talk to me in front of Becky. And she would stick near me after band period, which meant that we'd be together when Becky showed up to walk me to my next class.

"Later, man," Dharma would say, and then she would glide off, all sleek hips and long hair, and I would feel Becky's discomfort as we wobbled along after her.

Pretty soon the writing was clearly on the wall.

Becky got older-woman with me and said I was getting too friendly with Dharma, and I said we were just friends because of band, and Becky said I should tell her to back off, and I said that was silly, and Becky began to get sarcastic, and I got defensive, and then we outright quarreled.

Things went downhill from there, until one day Becky cornered me at my locker with a me-or-her ultimatum. When I only looked apologetically back at her, she brushed her eyes with the sleeve of her sweatshirt and waded away.

I knew I'd been a shithead for real. I never actually stopped caring about Becky O'Dell, or feeling guilty about doing her that way.

But I was a teenaged boy, full of juice, and I'd only recently been released from my long isolation, and none of that slowed me down with regard to Donna York.

Once we became a couple, it wasn't long before she made all those erotic promises come true. The first time was in the pine grove behind her house. Her parents lived in a big, gabled place on a property that had been cut out of the woods a mile from Baxter village.

It was two weeks after I'd broken up with Becky, and Donna had taken me there for a picnic lunch. She'd also grabbed a bottle of her mother's Chablis out of the fridge, and after a couple of glasses of wine and a lot of petting, she let me know the time had come by pushing me gently away, looking into my eyes, and unbuttoning her peasant blouse.

She leaned toward me concavely, so that the wide neck of the blouse fell off her shoulders, and gave me a moment to gape before crossing her arms to pull the blouse over her head. Then her pretty breasts were pointing my way, and she gave me another moment and fell into my arms.

Oh God: holding and kissing a girl with bare breasts! I lost my mind and forgot that this was just the preamble, and finally Donna had to push me away again, looking at me heavy-lidded and touching the tip of her tongue to her lip.

I ripped my jersey, yanking it over my head. We kicked our jeans off and quickly were naked. Donna lay back and reached for me; after I poked and missed a couple of times, she pushed me over onto my back, swung a leg over, and let herself exquisitely down onto me. I felt the incredible clutching softness of her, and she began moving and threw her head back. I held her waist and looked up at her breasts and the underside of her jaw and she kept moving and I never wanted it to stop.

But then she moaned, and that sound coming out of her because of me was too much. She kept moving, and moaned again, and my mind shattered. Then my mind came back together and she slowed and stopped, still clutching, and then she lay down flat against me and we held each other.

It was over too fast to have been very impressive to a worldly girl like Donna, but she sighed deeply as if I were indeed Don Juan, and softly kissed my neck.

"That was so far out, Cool," she said, which was the nickname she'd given me after we'd been together for a few days, because Cal, she said, was way too old-fashioned. ("I mean, it was the name of one of those old-time presidents, right?")

"Yeah," I said, and it *was* far out, not least because it had smoothed the last stubborn textures out of my mind, the tiny, furtive ones that were almost always lurking.

Lying there with her, I was at peace in a way I'd forgotten was possible. It was even better than beer, and afterwards, although I might have been embarrassed to be called "Cool," and I might have still felt ashamed about Becky, there was no chance at all that anything was going to go back to the way it had been.

Besides that, I was now a guy who had done it with a girl. I was a man, not a kid (good thing Pike wasn't standing in front of me), and that gave me a whole new persona to live up to, one which couldn't include someone like Becky.

Part of that persona required at least pretending to be Dharma's counterpart. And from then on we were Cool and Dharma, romantic and talented, and I have to admit that as phony as that often felt, it still seemed better than being Becky's puppy-love boyfriend, or a Shithead in Good Standing, or even some lesser member of the high school In-Crowd, like Alvin. (He'd gotten himself a grudging sort of acceptance by throwing me under the bus with the story about the barn, and he'd clung to that niche ever since by being the kid who laughed at everyone's jokes and played the piano at parties.)

I started reading the Beats, and Kurt Vonnegut, and James Baldwin, and my hair got longer, and after a couple of months, at Dharma's prompting, I splurged on bell-bottoms and a buckskin vest from my lawn-mowing cash.

At home things shifted again. Pike figured I was now a drug-addled hippie not worth the time of day. It also wasn't clear to either of us what might happen if we ever came nose to nose again, so we tried to avoid that possibility.

Becky didn't quite know what to make of the new me, but it didn't cause the problems it might have because graduation was a year closer, and we all knew I'd be saying good-bye soon (if I even bothered).

As for Alvin, he graduated early, got a job at Dad's old employer—sort of a legacy deal—and was never around the house anyway. Then he moved into an apartment with another of the car salesmen, and I never saw him at all.

Dharma and I spent that summer riding around in the Volkswagen Bug her daddy had bought her. She'd painted it with flowers and peace symbols, and we took it to protests and concerts and the coffeehouse in Rockland (Trouble Brewing, it was called), where one day we saw Alvin and his roommate on a field trip to observe hippies. (Alvin saw me come in and gave me a smirk, but didn't come over to talk.)

Oh, and we did a lot of drinking, Dharma and I.

We drank everywhere, pretty much. (She talked me into trying pot, but it brought out the old swirling meanies a little too vividly.) Her parents would rather she drank than *use drugs* anyway, and were cool with us having a glass or two at their house, which made it easy. (Probably too easy, considering my future lack of sobriety.)

I took her over to Uncle Gus's a couple of times, but though he thought she was okay, he loved Becky, and that came through clearly enough that we stopped going. (Also, Becky was still visiting him, and one day we met her coming out of his house, something none of us was happy about.)

So no Uncle Gus, but Dharma's parents were enlightened enough that I could sleep over there (supposedly in separate rooms, but nobody ever checked).

Then our senior year arrived, and we were still Cool and Dharma, only more so. We were small-puddle luminaries, despised by the more-conventional students, but admired as antiheroes by new-age freshmen and sophomores.

I remember sitting at a cafeteria table while Dharma lectured on My Lai and Kent State and the Pentagon Papers. (And nodding wisely in agreement, although I never actually dug into the issues like her; I was still a self-conscious wannabe—happy about the side benefits, but still, in my mind, mostly about jazz and the trumpet. They'd been everything to me when I needed them, and still seemed far more authentic than anything else did.)

That senior year went fast, and after it was through, everything changed once again. (Sometimes it seems my life has been just one key change after another.)

Dharma and I had a few weeks before she went off to Berkeley, and although she promised nothing would ever come between us, it wasn't long until she fell under the spell of one of that school's firebrand radicals, which brought an end to my second-ever romance.

With no Dharma, no Becky, and no school, I had to struggle not to revert to the Shithead I'd been.

I didn't want to even think about college; had been dying to be free of school for years. My dream was to apprentice somehow with a jazz-meister, but that would be hard to do in Maine. It was something to figure out down the road, after I'd settled into an adult existence somewhere.

It helped that I moved in full-time with Uncle Gus and joined a little jazz combo that he took around to nursing homes and Legion Halls. (Alvin, who still played the piano, joined us a couple of times, and there were actually moments when the salty old bond we'd once had briefly resurfaced.)

Drinking beer, and sex (when I could find it), continued to be reliable comforts. I'd gotten a stopgap job at the shoe shop in Emery Falls, pushing racks of half-made shoes around the dim old building, and the guys I rode to work with didn't mind stopping at Blackstone's Market on the way home and buying me a six-pack, so I had a steady supply of that, anyway.

One thing I didn't have to worry about was Vietnam, because I'd gotten a high number in the draft lottery, so with no need for a school deferment (fake hippie or not, I wasn't going to involve myself voluntarily in that mess), I had time to try and figure things out.

Over the course of a couple of months I decided that when I'd saved enough money for a grubstake, I'd move to Portland and see what was up there. It wouldn't be a radical departure—I'd still be in Maine—but it would be in a city with a lot more going on than Baxter.

I waited until I had five hundred bucks—a decent amount back in the day—and then I did stop in to the old farmhouse on the river to say good-bye, making sure Pike would be at work. (Unfortunately this meant Alvin would also be at work; after the gigs with Uncle Gus, I wouldn't have minded shaking his hand and saying adios.)

My mother was sitting on the porch, reading the newspaper, smoking a cigarette. She was still a good-looking woman, although there were crow's feet at the corners of her eyes now, and erosion starting to show on her cheeks. She'd gone partly gray over the past couple of years, too.

"Hey," I said, laying my bike down, climbing the steps.

"Hello, Cal." She put her newspaper aside. "It's been a while."

"Yeah." We both knew why; nobody had to spell it out.

"So," I said, "I'm leaving town; thought I'd come over and say good-bye."

"Leaving for where?"

"Portland, to start with."

She nodded. "Clean slate, huh?"

"That's what I figure."

We looked at each other, and all at once I could see the younger Betty in her face, and it started me thinking about what it had been like when Julie and my father were still around, before everything turned to crap. Maybe she was thinking that, too, because after a moment she stubbed the cigarette out and stood up to give me a stiff little hug.

"I hope things work out for you, Calvin."

"That makes two of us."

We managed to smile, and that was pretty much that.

I said, "Tell Alvin I said good-bye," then walked down the steps, grabbed my bike, and set off along the driveway. When I got to the barn I looked over my shoulder, and she was still sitting in the rocker, watching.

I waved and she waved back.

I pedaled past the barn and down to the River Road and started up the long incline to Uncle Gus's. I had a last night there—he broke out a six-pack of his prized Woodchuck Hard Cider, and we drank it listening to Clark Terry—and in the morning he gave me a ride into town—the river, the village buildings, the tall flagpole by the town office, the little park with the Civil War monument—and pulled over by the Route 1 bridge just south of Baxter.

There was a shower passing through, so we sat in his used Buick to wait it out. He hadn't gotten any slimmer and took up a lot of room in the front seat, and it got a little claustrophobic with him clearing his throat and drumming his fingers on the steering wheel.

He finally looked over at me and said, "Shoot me a note when you get settled in?"

"Sure. I'll give you the lowdown."

"We're gonna miss you in the band."

"I'll miss it, too."

"You can sit in when you visit."

"Sure!"

We watched the rain on the windshield. I could tell he had more to say, but he couldn't seem to spit it out; he just sat there with his face getting redder. It was never easy for Uncle Gus to talk about anything.

When the shower passed I shook his hand and came away with a fifty he'd pushed into my palm.

"Come on, Uncle G," I said, but he wouldn't take it back, and I shook his hand again and got out of the car.

I grabbed my stuff out of the backseat, shut the door, and stepped back to the shoulder. He waited for traffic, then pulled a U-turn and saluted going past, and I watched him cruise back toward Baxter on the wet road.

Past him I could see the outskirts of the little town. I took a deep breath: This was something I'd been looking forward to since Pike had stuck his snout into our lives, and now it was happening. It was exciting, but also made me a little nervous, and when a few bat-like shadows decided to come alive in my head I dug a beer out of the duffel, walked down behind the guardrail onto the riverbank, and chugged it. Then I tossed the empty into the water and climbed back up.

I stuck my thumb out and tried to make eye contact as each vehicle approached. The first few ignored me as they swept past. But the fifth one that came along—a black Ford Ranger—slowed as soon as he saw me and pulled over.

I trotted up to the passenger side and looked in the window. He was an amiable-looking guy only a little older than me. He wore a Red Sox cap and a canvas duck jacket, and there was a carpenter's tool chest built into the back of the truck, and some power tools loose on the floor.

"Hop in," he said. "Where you heading?"

"Portland, if you're going that far."

"You're in luck."

I threw the duffel into the back and climbed into the front seat with my instrument case.

He stuck out his hand. "Raymond Lane."

"Cal Shaw."

He nodded at the case. "That's not a machine gun, is it?"

"Just a trumpet."

"I guess that's all right."

"Hold on." I got out and leaned over the side of the cargo bed to pull the rest of the six-pack out of the bag. Back in the front he took one and stuck it between his legs. Then he looked over his shoulder and spun the tires, scooting onto the road ahead of a bulky dump truck.

I probably would have waited, myself.

We accelerated across the bridge, and when the dump truck began falling back instead of gaining on us, he settled in, held the wheel with his knees while he twisted the cap off his bottle, and held the bottle out for me to click it against mine.

We drank and he turned up the radio—which had been quietly playing country-and-western music the whole time—and we charged down the road away from Baxter. When we got to Damariscotta we opened another couple of beers.

It was turning into a fine morning, all the low scud blown through and the sun out. The sun climbed into the sky behind us as we rode past the little towns on Route 1, and in Bath we cracked two more beers and clicked them together.

The sun got higher, while in front our shadow got shorter. It had disappeared altogether by the time we passed the B&M Baked Beans plant and crossed the bridge into Portland.

Raymond Lane dropped me on Marginal Way, and drove off beeping his horn. I knew I'd never see him again, which made me a little sad because we'd had a good time.

I walked across Forest Avenue to Deering Oaks and sat in the open on a park bench. The sun was warm and high now overhead, and there were pretty girls walking the park paths and squirrels running between trees. Dignified geese were swimming in the pond. Everything was bathed in a warm glow, thanks to the beer. It was really the first time I'd gotten buzzed like that in the morning, and I decided I liked it quite a lot. It was another restriction gone.

I nodded to myself, lit one more cigarette, and drew in the smoke, looking around at my new town, my new life.

TAKE A QUICK BREAK, BROTHER

THIRTY

Bolduc Correctional Facility, 1997

So a lot happened in the next fifteen years that I could talk about. There was the little rooming house on Valley Street, where I spent the first of those years, whose proprietor—an old-timer named Tate Cummings—told me about living in Harlem and listening to Ornette Coleman and Clifford Brown and Wayne Shorter at the clubs.

There was the Pancake Kitchen on Congress Street, where I met Jack Doyle—trombonist and cabbie—who not only took me to the all-night club on State Street and introduced me to most of Portland's little jazz community, but also got me in at Norman Finkelstein's Star of David Taxi Service, where I learned the town as only a cabbie can: the bums sleeping on cardboard under the Million Dollar Bridge; the Shaw's on Congress where the register girls would come out and flirt; the Dunkin Donuts on Congress and High where in winter the working girls would spike-heel over to warm up in your cab; the pipeline in South Portland where you could bootleg for the sailors on Sunday.

Driving a taxi turned out to be one thing I was good at besides the trumpet, and also allowed me to support myself while I got going musically.

I remember my first trips to the Free Street Pub on Middle Street, where on Wednesday Jazz Night I'd sit in with the people I'd met at the all-night club—which led to actual gigs there and at Mordecai's on outer Congress and the Top of the East in the Eastland Hotel and

Little Willie's on Market Street . . . which in turn got me invited to Don Doane's jam sessions at the Bridgeway in South Portland, and later to fill-in gigs with his orchestra . . . which eight years along—it went fast!—got me a letter of introduction from Mr. Doane to his old friend Bradley Cunningham in NYC . . . which got me a job bartending at Bradley's, where you could listen to some of the biggest names around—think Freddie Hubbard, just starting out—and even sit in with them after hours in the back room after they'd gotten to like you enough to believe you were serious.

There are a thousand things I could tell you about Portland, and then another thousand about New York, and along the way I could fill you in on my drinking career and how I slid from self-medicating boy to party animal to mostly functioning alcoholic, to not-doing-so-well *sot*, to the drunken mess who staggered out of the Big Apple for Florida with a girl named Gigi Archambeau, who smartly ditched me once we got there.

I'd truly like to try and tell you all that. Maybe I will some time. But I'm not sure I'm up to it just now.

IT JUST DEPENDS

THIRTY-ONE

En Route, 1995

Loretta McCarty, Georgie and I spend about twenty hours together, asleep and awake, stopping in Richmond and Baltimore, playing with the cornet when we have a chance. I decide Georgie is serious enough to learn about false fingering, how to get around the edict that you must never play any note using the third valve by itself, how if you ignore that nonsense you can go right up a high-note C scale without playing a single two- or three-valve position (which does leave some notes a shade off, but that's true of the trumpet in general, and all you have to do is listen to Louis Armstrong's intro to "West End Blues" to know that it works anyway).

Georgie is worried to go there at first, but while we're in Baltimore I convince him to at least give it a try, and after playing for a while on a bench outside the station, he decides he likes it. He feels bold and a bit naughty, too—you can see it in his eyes—and by the time we have to re-board the bus, he's become something of a convert.

Who knows if it'll last, but it makes all of us happy for the time being, and we ride the rest of the way to Boston like friends—so much so that when the bus finally pulls into South Station and we have to go our separate ways, it's unsettling. I feel like there's been an interlude that's coming to an end.

We wait in our seats while the other passengers squeeze down the aisle, and then Loretta takes a notebook out of her purse and writes down Georgie's home address and phone number—he lives in Chelsea—and hers, back in Plant City.

I give them the phone number of the farmhouse in Baxter, but say I'm not sure whether I'll actually be staying there when all is said and done.

"You're not going to stay at home?"

"It just depends on how things go."

She touches my arm and says, "I'm sorry it's like that, Calvin," and just like that I get choked up. I've been holding it off since we got to Boston, but a kind touch has always rendered me pretty much helpless.

"It'll be all right, honey," she says. "Just don't make up your mind in advance. You never know for sure what's going to happen."

I swallow and say, "Uh-huh."

"Promise you'll give me a call when you're back in Tampa."

"I will," I manage to say, but I'm afraid it won't actually happen, that we'll just have been ships passing, et cetera, and that makes it even worse.

When Georgie says, "You can call me too," I can't even speak, but I hold my hand out so he can high-five me, which he does in his own unique way, kind of like a karate tap.

They wriggle out of their seats and walk down the aisle, and after a last smile from Loretta at the top of the little stairwell, they climb down off the bus.

Through the tinted window I watch them walk away. It gives me a certain feeling; like Raymond Lane and a few others, they're people who have flicked through my orbit that I'll likely never see again, but who I know will be in my mind off and on forever.

A few minutes later there's a knock on the bus door. A man in a tan uniform steps up to say something low to our driver. He leaves and our driver walks back to tell me and two others also waiting that we're switching buses for the last part of the run up to Portland.

"How come?" I say.

He lifts his shoulders. "Ours is not to reason why."

I get off and grab my duffel when he unloads it onto the pavement. There's some time to kill now, and I use the facilities, buy a couple of Snickers bars to get me through the last leg, and then find the gate for my next ride.

We have the same driver for this bus, which is newer than our old one, and after he loads our baggage we climb up the steps past the fan mounted on the dash above the WATCH YOUR STEP sign and sidle down the aisle.

I take a place about halfway back. The seats—two on each side of the aisle—are plush compared to the bus we started with. It's overcast and dark, and with a half-hour to wait, I recline my seat the few inches it allows and shut my eyes. I get drowsy right away—it's been a long ride—and my mind drifts between thoughts of Baxter and home and Portland and Uncle Gus, all hooked up to his machinery. The different shades of these thoughts mingle into a smoky sort of blend, and I go a long way away, and the next thing I know the driver is standing next to me, asking to see my ticket, as if we hadn't been riding together for the past however many miles.

"Seriously?"

"Protocol." He shrugs.

I fumble in my pockets, then squeeze out of my seat—the driver stepping back—and finally I manage to find it in my back pocket.

He gives it a cursory glance and hands it back.

I sit back down and he works his way to the last seats next to the lavatory and then returns to the front and plops down in his seat.

He yawns and stretches, toggles switches like a jet pilot, then levers the door open to see if anyone is waiting to board. There's no one there and he shuts the door, checks his wristwatch, and cranks the engine.

There's a slight lurch when he puts the bus in gear.

I look at my watch too and try to figure when I'll get to Portland. My stomach clenches at the thought, and I can feel the anxiety jittering through my body.

More than twenty years, and almost over.

We back out of the parking space and pull forward away from the boarding gate and then we're moving down the street, heading for the Interstate.

LOOK WHAT THE
CAT DRAGGED IN

THIRTY-TWO

Portland, 1995

I try to doze again during the ride, but it just doesn't happen, I'm too nerved up. My little drink demon is whispering sweet nothings in my ear; fortunately, there's no way for me to fall off the wagon while I'm on this bus. Then the notion to sneak a cigarette in the lavatory crawls into my mind. But I hold off there, as well. I don't really want to ruin my sober return to Maine by acting like some kind of punk.

So I stay put, watching out the window, checking the time.

The two-hour ride seems to take forever.

Finally, though, we cut through Portsmouth and cross the high-arcing Piscataqua River Bridge into Maine. I sit up straight: It feels momentous.

Through the window the pine trees look friendly and familiar, and like a good omen the overcast is tattering away, the sun peeking through tones of grayness here and there.

I pull my cornet case out and hold it in my lap, and as we roll up I-95 I whisper to this New York instrument; I tell it all about Maine.

We cruise up to Portland, skipping past the small towns— Kennebunkport, Biddeford, Saco, Scarborough—and then we sort of burst out of the spring-green woods to the sprawling Maine Mall and the roundhouse Dunfey Hotel, and I know we're getting close.

We exit the turnpike and go cross-country for a couple of miles, and then we swoop down to the Veterans Bridge and cross the Fore

River. Ahead I can see the Maine Medical Center on the Western Prom bluff—a mix of old gothic spires and new brick walls—and I think about Uncle G lying in his hospital bed. Then we're off the bridge and slowing past the old brick railroad offices and turning into the low-built Greyhound station.

We snub up against the padded stop-guard next to the double doors. The driver sets our luggage on the pavement, tells us to enjoy our visit to Portland and walks off, lighting a smoke.

It's sunny out now, and warm for May. I walk over to check out the Star of David taxi parked by the curb, but the driver is no one I know, which doesn't surprise me, since it's been a decade now, and the turnover rate for cabbies is never low.

"Need a cab, buddy?" he says.

"Just wondering how old Norman's doing."

"Not too good," This cabbie is chewing gum and smoking at the same time, flicking the ash out his window every few seconds.

"Is he sick?"

"Dead," the cabbie says, looking up at me.

"What happened?"

"The diabetes got him."

"I'm sorry to hear that."

He shrugs, flicks ash. He's not exactly all broken up over Finkelstein's demise.

"Did you drive for him at all?"

"For about a week."

"Who's running the show now?"

"His kid, Bugsy."

"Well, tell him Cal Shaw said hi, would you?"

There's a call on his radio before he can answer. He grabs the mike and says, "Roger," hangs the mike back up by its clip, starts his cab, says, "Watch your toes," and drives off.

"Nice meeting you, too," I say.

Then I hoist the duffel over my shoulder, pick up the cornet case, and set off walking up Congress Street. I look at the familiar buildings and signs and side streets—even the people seem like people I should know—and all kinds of little memory shapes dart and swarm around me.

I pass Valley Street, but the rooming house where I lived all those years before is gone, just a weedy lot there now. Old Tate must have passed on—he was in his eighties when I knew him—and maybe there wasn't anyone to take over.

Then I'm opposite the Sportsman's Grill, where I ate spaghetti-and-meat-sauce meals, and consumed gallons of house wine—I remember how I'd leave there and walk on air down the street to Tate's—and I continue on up to the old Rines Mansion (the Roma Café, another favored watering hole, in its basement) and turn right on Bramhall, past the nurses' housing, and I keep climbing toward the Medical Center.

By the time I finally reach the entrance I have to stop in the lobby and set the duffel down to catch my breath. Then I step up to the reception desk to get directions to Uncle Gus's room. I ask the lady there if I can leave my bag with her, but she tells me they're not allowed to be responsible for people's things.

So I tow it to the elevator and ride up to the ICU. There's a large woman at the nurses' station with big round glasses and a quick smile. She confirms Uncle Gus's room number, tells me how to find it, and then says, "You can leave your bag here if you don't want to haul it around."

"I tried that downstairs."

She rolls her eyes and flutters a hand. Then she gets up from her chair and opens the little waist-high door so I can slide the duffel bag in.

"I'll keep the horn with me."

"Are you going to play for him?"

"Is that allowed?"

She pretends to whisper behind her hand. "I won't tell if you don't."

"If I do I'll be quiet."

She gives me a thumbs-up, plops back down in her seat.

I take the long corridor to the left of the nurses' station and walk almost to the end.

Everything's in warm colors; there are paintings on the walls, and a big window at the end that lets the light in. It's not that bad for a hospital.

Uncle Gus's door is open, and at first I think they've given me the wrong room. Or maybe the guy lying asleep in there is the roommate. But then I register the bird's-nest eyebrows and potato nose, and I know it's him. He's lost weight, and most of his hair. He has big, pallid bags under his eyes. His eyes are shut, and he's breathing with his mouth open.

There's an intravenous rack with a tube that runs down to his arm; also, a complicated-looking machine on a shelf behind him, with wires connected to the back of his left hand. The machine is beeping and clicking. There's a glass of water with a straw on the side table.

I'm still in the doorway, a sickly, greenish shape rolling through my mind, and for a moment I'm not sure I'll be able to get myself to move any closer.

But I force a foot forward, then the other, and it loosens me up enough that I can walk in and set the cornet case down next to a folding chair beside his bed.

Uncle Gus doesn't seem to notice my arrival.

I sit down to wait, feeling bad about my poor job of keeping in touch. (I had good intentions, and did call a couple of times, but we were never that proficient at small-talking with one another, and it was always awkward.)

"I'll do better if you get better," I tell him, and he stops halfway into an inhalation. At first I'm happy that he might have reacted to me, but the pause lasts a long time, until I stand up, ready to run for help, but finally he resumes breathing with a little gasp, and after watching for another minute, I sit back down.

I've been there for an hour when a young nurse comes in, looking about nineteen but giving off an air of efficiency and capability.

"Hello!" she says. "Are you here to see Augustus? Oh, he's one of my favorites." She bends over Uncle Gus and says, "Aren't you, honey?" Then she looks at me again. "Are you another nephew?"

"Uh-huh," I say. "Sort of."

She cocks her head a little at that, but doesn't comment. She takes Uncle Gus's pulse, checks the fluid level in the intravenous bag, twiddles a couple of dials on the monitor on the shelf, then walks back and jots something on the clipboard at the foot of the bed.

"How's he doing?"

"About as well as can be expected." She hangs the clipboard back on its hook. "He's been through a lot, poor man. He's a fighter, though."

"My brother thought he was pretty aware of things."

"He's had a little setback. Haven't you, Augustus?"

I lower my voice. "Is he in a coma?"

She answers in the same kind of voice. "Not exactly."

"What does that mean?"

"He's sort of in between."

"Do you think he can hear us?"

"It's hard to say."

She leans over the bed and says, "Bye, Augustus; you behave yourself now," and with a quick smile scoots out of the room and heads off down the corridor.

I sit a while longer, but it makes me uneasy, watching Uncle Gus, and I get up and walk past the divider curtain to the window. There's an old brick spire with gabled rooftops around it and a courtyard way down at ground level. There are a couple of interns down in the courtyard, smoking.

I go back and sit down again, take the paperback out of my hip pocket, and try to read, but there are ripples of feelings bouncing around Uncle Gus—mine or his, I'm not sure which—and they're roiling the air. It's hard to concentrate.

I close the book and look at him again. He needs a shave, and a lot of the stubble is white. His eyelids are twitching as if he might be dreaming.

I wonder if I should leave and come back, maybe head out to Baxter and get that over with, then return and see if anything's changed.

But I can't decide, so I try the book again, and after I force myself through a couple of paragraphs, it goes easier. I'm right there with this space orphan raised by Martians and ghosts when the young nurse comes back in and tells me apologetically that visiting time is over for that afternoon.

I go back to the nurses' station for my duffel.

"Did you play for him?" the nice lady asks.

"Not yet."

"I listened for you."

"Maybe when I come back."

She gives me another thumbs-up.

I ride the elevator down, and after thinking it over in the lobby, decide I'm not ready for Baxter, so I lug my gear the seven or eight blocks to Forest Avenue and down the hill to the YMCA. They have a transient room available, so I fork over a few bucks and stow my gear. I spend the rest of that afternoon and the next few days revisiting old haunts between trips to the hospital.

The Pancake Kitchen is still in business, and one morning after breakfast there I set out to find Jack Doyle, but he's not at the hole-in-the-wall apartment on Cumberland Avenue, and when I hike over to Little Willie's, they tell me he hasn't been around for a few years now.

"Any idea where he went?"

"Back to New York, I think."

I hit the Old Port—which I liked better in my day, because it was full of artists and musicians—and wander down to Commercial Street—nodding at Blake's Plumbing Supply, where I had a warehouse job for a little while—and then I hike all the way up Munjoy Hill to the Eastern Promenade, where we'd play drunken softball on Sunday afternoons.

I'm enjoying being in Portland again, but by that Saturday, with no change in Uncle Gus, I decide I might as well get Baxter over with. I've thought about skipping it altogether, but that would be weak, and I'm trying to be strong.

I check out of the Y, lug my stuff over to the Medical Center and tell Uncle Gus all this, and that I'll be back to see him again after I'm done in Baxter. Then I ask his advice as to whether I should call Alvin for a ride or hike down to Marginal Way and stick out my thumb.

He doesn't answer, so I mull it over on my own, and have pretty much decided to make the call and suffer the third degree. Then it's only inertia keeping me there until someone taps politely on the door and comes walking into the room.

I look up expecting to see the young nurse, but there's a tallish woman standing there instead, leaning on a cane, wearing a faded blue SMVTI T-shirt and jeans and a Red Sox cap over a thick shock of chestnut hair.

Her eyes widen, and I recognize her at the same time, but my tongue is tied just long enough for her to speak first.

"Well, look what the cat dragged in," she says.

THIRTY-THREE

Portland, 1995

She comes into the room, and it takes me a second to realize something: She might be using a cane, but she's not knock-kneed. She's standing up straight like I've never seen her before.

"Hey!" I stand up too and point at her legs.

She stops to bow and sweep an arm out—which is funny in itself, Becky O'Dell curtsying—and then comes the rest of the way over to the bed.

I step aside and gesture her toward the chair, mimicking her curtsy, and she smiles as she sits down.

"Back again, Uncle G," she says, and lowers her pocketbook to the floor.

"It's nice you come to see him."

"He's my friend."

"Do you mind if I stick around?"

"It's a free country."

I grab another chair from behind the curtain and plunk it down beside her. She takes Uncle G's hand and studies his face, looking for signs of life. She ignores me until I lean forward and say, "I think I should apologize."

"Nah, forget it," she says.

"I've always wanted to."

"I'd rather not talk about it." She taps the cornet case with her cane. "So have you played for him?"

"Yeah, a couple of times."

"Did anything happen?"

"Maybe. It's hard to tell."

"Try it again so I can see."

She turns back to Uncle Gus, ready to watch closely. There are flecks of gray in her hair, which is otherwise as thick and pretty as ever, and her skin still has that outdoor ruddiness that always made her seem so healthy.

"Anytime now," she says.

I take out the cornet, fit the amber mouthpiece in, and flutter the valves. I stick my fingers into the bell and play the first few bars of "Blue Summer," soft as I can manage.

Nothing happens, though.

"One more time."

I shut my eyes and take it up to the bridge, willing it into Uncle Gus's mind, wanting Becky to hear it, too.

"There!" she says.

I stop and look.

Becky is leaning close. "That was something."

"What'd he do?"

"Something in his face."

"His eyes?"

"His whole face."

I play a little more, watching this time, but whatever it was doesn't repeat, and when Becky says, "I guess he's being difficult, now," I put the cornet away. We get back to watching him, and after a little while I say, "So tell me about the cane."

"Nah." She pats Uncle Gus's hand.

"Come on, tell me."

"Why would you care?"

"Because I do."

She laughs under her breath, then shrugs one shoulder and rattles it off: "Broke my leg on the boat, got tangled up in a trawl line, and almost went overboard. Slammed my leg into the transom to stop it and ended up with a spiral fracture, had three operations and a cast for almost a year."

"Jeez," I say, "when was this?"

"Four or five years after you took off."

"What happened then?"

She shrugs again like it's nothing.

"When the cast came off I had to learn to walk all over again, and I guess this time I managed to learn the right way."

"How long did that take?"

"Another year."

"That's amazing!"

Another shrug.

"Come on, you must have felt like a new person."

"Oh yeah," she says. "A regular Donna York."

I wait while that rattles around in my head.

Becky clears her throat, stares at Uncle Gus.

Finally I say, "Listen, I was a shit, but it wasn't because of your legs."

"If you say so."

"I do say so."

"Good, I'm glad we got that cleared up."

She still won't look at me.

"I was sixteen, Becky."

"So what?"

"Sixteen-year-old boys don't know anything."

She looks at me, finally.

"I've always been really, really sorry."

"All right."

"I mean it."

"I said all right."

"Friends?" I stick out my hand.

"Let's not get carried away."

I can't help feeling a little stricken at this, and I guess it shows in my face, because her own softens a bit. But then her chin comes up and she says, "Nope, don't even try."

"What?"

"Making me feel bad."

"I could burst into tears."

This almost gets me one of her old crooked grins. She swallows it quickly, but I can tell. Then she says, "You're pathetic, Cal Shaw," and this is so much like what she would have said twenty years before that it makes both of us laugh.

Becky shakes her head and looks back at Uncle Gus.

I tell her what Alvin had said, and she agrees that when she first came to see him he was definitely awake and could let you know he was listening.

"He'd give my hand a squeeze, wouldn't you, Uncle G?"

Uncle Gus breathes steadily and gives no sign, and after a few minutes we settle back, and now everything has changed and we're just hanging out together with him.

Then Becky says, "So what have you been up to?"

We spend the next hour swapping stories. I pick up where she left off, tell her about driving a taxi in Portland and playing around town, about Don Doane and Bradley Cunningham and getting started in New York, and my musical career there, such as it was, and I describe lighting out for Tampa and driving a taxi there, too, and playing at Hendu's the night Alvin called.

She tells me how her father wanted to finish setting the traps before steaming in and how he waited another day before taking her to see a doctor. "He never had any money," she says. Then she talks about using her convalescent time to get a two-year fisheries degree, and how afterwards she took a job at the same lobster co-op where her old man traded.

"He had a new stern man by then, anyway. And I liked it at the co-op. Still do. I'm around boats and outdoors, but I don't have to work as hard, and I'm not quite so *aromatic* when I get home, either."

"What about the cane?"

She says that sometimes her hips get tender, which is a result of using them wrong all those years. It's nothing much, she says. "Just something that comes and goes."

We decide to run for coffee.

I tell Uncle Gus we'll be right back, grab my horn, and we head down the corridor. We pass the desk with a wave for the nice nurse, and at the elevator Becky presses the down button and I watch the floor numbers light up above the door.

The elevator dings and the door slides open.

On the first floor we walk along another corridor to the cafeteria. The counter is closed, but there are vending machines, and we buy cups of muddy coffee and carry them to a table by the windows that look out at Vaughn Street.

I set the cornet case down and take a seat.

"You still carry that everywhere?"

"Pretty much."

"I guess it's good you're still playing."

"Yeah, most of the time."

I smirk, remembering when it wasn't so good—how during one epic binge I convinced myself I was Bix Beiderbecke come back to life, and how I decided to let everyone else in on the news by having a one-man show in downtown Tampa at two o'clock in the morning, and how in the ensuing fracas with the cops I took a wild swing at one of them with my cornet, which was enough for them to charge me with assault in addition to my other offenses.

I'm trying to get another laugh from her, but Becky doesn't think it's very funny, so I move quickly on to the kick tank at Pinellas and getting sober despite myself.

"Good for you," she says. "How's that going?"

"All right. Ups and downs."

"I know it's not easy."

Turns out her brother went to AA a few years back, and she sat in on the meetings to try and help, because his wife had left him and he didn't have anyone else.

"He didn't last, though. Decided he liked drinking too much."

"I know the feeling."

"It used to sneak up on him."

"Yeah. It's insidious. You get clearheaded and start feeling strong, and that makes you think you're all better and you can handle having a drink or two."

We get back on the subject of Uncle Gus, and reminisce about how we'd hang out at his place when I had my lessons, and how later we would dodge each other coming and going.

"I lived with him, too, for a while."

"You did?"

"After I got divorced."

"You were married?"

"Believe it or not."

She tells me that they'd been living at her husband's parents' house, and when they split she thought she was doomed to move back in with her own parents, but then she bumped into Uncle Gus at the Esso station.

"I was crying on his shoulder, and he just up and offered me the guest room."

"Sounds like him."

"Doesn't it?"

"Did it spark a few rumors?"

"You know Baxter, silly as it was. But we didn't care."

She lived there for almost a year, but dropped in often even after she'd moved into a little apartment over the hardware store in the downtown block.

"And you've stayed single."

"Yeah, I learned my lesson."

"What lesson is that?"

"Guys are shits," she says. "Sixteen or not. But now I don't worry about it. It is what it is, and you just have to realize that and not let yourself get too carried away."

"You sound kind of cynical."

"It's the new me."

We sip our coffee and look out the window at the street. It's rush hour and there's a lot of traffic, and I remember counting cars with Becky and Julie, and when I bring that up—and board games and croquet, and playing in the barn—Becky gets misty-eyed and blows her nose on a napkin.

"Julie's still the best friend I ever had. That's probably what made it so bad about you: I thought you were going to be the next best thing."

"I wish I had been."

"You're a guy."

"Some of us must be all right."

"You couldn't prove it by me."

She holds up her hand with its unadorned ring finger.

"Same kind of deal as with you, Cal. You're all hopeless. The grass is always greener or some darn thing. What got me about Scott was that it was after my broken leg and all that. I wasn't even damaged goods!"

"When did this happen?"

"Six years and . . . two months ago."

I hold up my own bare-fingered hand.

"Divorced?"

"Never took the plunge."

"How come?"

"I *was always* damaged goods."

She gives me a funny look, then laughs. "Well, that's over with."

"You deserved better."

"*Now* he gets it."

She grins, but it's a slippery one, because she's still weepy about Julie, and now about me too again, and seeing that vulnerability, my heart makes a sudden wobble in her direction. But that's plain silly.

It's been a long time, and besides, I'm still drying out, and no prize for anyone.

So I make some pitiful joke about finally being old enough to figure out one or two things, and she snorts and says, "I'll believe it when I see it," and we look out the window again, and I finally break down and ask about my mother and Pike, and she says, "Still going strong, as far as I can tell."

We finish our coffee and go back up to Uncle Gus's room.

He's cranked up to a sitting position, with the young nurse helping him eat chocolate pudding. She touches his lips lightly with the spoon, and when he opens his mouth, wipes the pudding off on his lip.

"I told Augustus you were here. I'm not sure he heard, but he's in there somewhere, aren't you, honey?" She gives him another taste. "He's got an eating reflex, anyway."

She feeds him the whole container, then pats his chin and mouth with a damp cloth, gathers up the container, the lid, and the spoon, and stands up from the chair.

"When do we have to clear out?"

"You still have some time. I'll be back later." She smiles on her way out of the room.

"There's a girl for you," Becky says.

"That baby?"

"That baby was checking you out."

"If you say so."

Uncle Gus touches his lips with his tongue. His face is still impassive. He feels around and then stops. Then he takes a big breath, holds it a moment, and lets it out.

We stay with him for another hour, talking about Baxter, trying to do it in a way that includes him, just in case he might be listening.

Becky tells me that when she sees Pike and my mother around town, they never speak to her, and then the baby nurse comes back in to tell us visiting hours are over.

At the nurses' station I grab my duffel.

"Did you play for him this time?"

"A little."

"I thought I heard something!"

We're riding down in the elevator when Becky says, "How long are you here for?"

"I'm not sure."

"Are you coming back tomorrow?"

I tell her it depends on what happens in Baxter.

"You're going out there today?"

"Figured I'd better."

"Do you have a ride?"

"No, but I'm working on it."

We reach the first floor and the door opens. I follow her past the desk to the exit. Outside she faces me, and I notice we're almost eye to eye now that she can stand up straight.

"I suppose I ought to give you a ride."

"You don't have to do that."

"I'm going there anyway."

An ambulance comes up Bramhall Street and swings toward the Emergency entrance. I hope it's a good sign for someone that its lights and siren aren't on. It disappears around the corner and I look back at Becky.

"Well?" she says.

"I wouldn't have to call Alvin."

"That's reason enough."

She starts off, barely letting the cane touch the ground.

I shoulder the duffel and follow her across the street. When she gets to the other side she turns and tells me I can stop lagging and watching her walk anytime.

"Sorry."

"You're sorry all right."

She waits until I've caught up and sets off again. At her Silverado I put my bag in the back with various buckets and tubs, then climb up into the passenger seat.

In ten minutes we're turning off Franklin onto Marginal Way, and then we're crossing Back Cove, cruising past the baked beans factory and heading down Route 1.

"So which Scott did you marry, anyway?"

"Not one you'd know."

She tells me he was from one of the islands, a lobster buyer, and they were hitched for about a year and a half before he started cheating on her with a barmaid from the Old Port. Then she asks me if I'd heard about Alvin quitting the dealership and going to work for Pike at the realty.

"No, I hadn't heard that."

"I'm surprised he never told you."

"We haven't been in touch, really."

Next she tells me Chuck Lamar and Bobby Berube joined the Marines together the year after we graduated, and that Bobby was killed during boot camp in some kind of training accident. I couldn't believe I hadn't heard about that, but it just goes to show you how out of touch I'd been.

"Aw, man."

"I know. I liked that little twerp."

Riding down 295, she fills me in on other notable goings-on in Baxter. She makes it funny, and before I know it we're crossing the Route 1 bridge into Baxter. Then we're riding down Main Street and I spot Chief Foss in his cruiser by the big flagpole.

"Don't tell me he's still around."

"Yeah, and just as dumb as ever."

He doesn't spot me, or he'd probably hit the lights and come after us for old times' sake.

We turn down Water Street to the bridge, and I start to feel the ghosts stirring, and then we thump off on the other side and another mile along come up to where my father had his accident. And even though you can't tell anymore that anything ever happened there, I get a jolt that shoots right up through all the other little jolts this visit has produced, and things start boiling around in my head.

It's more powerful than I expected, as well as I'd been doing. But those old shapes and colors have always had a way of jumping out to surprise me, and I suppose I should have known they wouldn't stop now.

I figure I'll just let it ride itself out, as usual, but the closer we get to the old farmhouse, the worse it becomes. By the time we pass Uncle Gus's I'm feeling pretty well surrounded and trapped, and I guess I'm not doing a very good job of hiding it, because all at once Becky slows and pulls over onto the shoulder.

"What is it?" I say through the bedlam.

"You were making a noise."

"What kind of noise?"

"Some kind of groan."

I try to laugh. "Are you sure I wasn't just humming?"

"You don't hum, Cal, you whistle."

"Sometimes I hum."

"You weren't this time, trust me."

I shake my head. "I'm sorry, Beck."

"Don't be sorry.

"We went by Dad's spot."

"I figured."

"That, and everything else."

"Uh-huh." She nods in the direction of my former home. "So are you sure about this? Because I've been thinking. I still have a key to Uncle G's. Why couldn't you stay there tonight, let yourself settle down a little."

"You mean go over in the morning?"

"Yeah."

I try to think it through, but it's still too noisy in my old bean, and Becky watches me struggle with it for a minute or two and then just goes ahead and throws the truck into gear, pulls a U-turn, and heads back toward the sun just setting below the trees between us and the village.

"I guess I've decided, huh?"

"I guess you have."

We pull into Uncle Gus's driveway. The house hasn't changed at all except the shingles are more weathered, and there's a copper trumpet weathervane on top of the one-car garage. Becky throws the gearshift and says, "Do you want me to come in?"

And I *do* want her to come in. Some trace of our old bond seems to be trying to breathe itself back to life, and I'm afraid if I let her get away that'll be the end of it. But I also know that in my present state I'm liable to do something stupid to kill it off anyway.

It's a tough call when you're not thinking clearly. But then I realize I'm taking too long to decide, which might hurt Becky's feelings all over again, and I can't take a chance about that so I say, "Yeah, please, I wish you would," and after hesitating for only an instant she shuts the engine off and we get out of her pickup and go into the house through the side door.

FOOLISH

THIRTY-FOUR

Baxter, 1995

Playing chords on the piano can be soothing—something about the way they resolve themselves—so I head right down to the basement to see if it'll help. Uncle Gus was still teaching right up until his stroke, and his studio hasn't changed much. It still has the paneling and the carpet and the drop ceiling with its smoke-discolored space above his recliner, and the same upright piano and the other instruments on their stands, and the student desks.

I sit down at the keyboard and noodle a little of "Blue Summer," using Tampa Red–style chords and a single-note melody line. It's actually the only tune I can bring into my head at that moment.

"That's what you played for Uncle Gus." Becky is sitting at one of the student desks.

"Yep." I play a little more, wanting her to hear it, and that stirs something in my mind, a possibility, but there's still a commotion up there—furtive shapes and dark colors—and I can't really focus.

I stop so as not to use it up and lose it.

I get up from the piano and smile at Becky and we wander back up the stairs.

In the kitchen she fires up the coffeemaker and we take a couple of mugs into the living room. On the couch we sip the hot coffee in unison, lower the mugs and look at each other.

"Unbelievable," Becky says.

"Back at Uncle Gus's."

"How are you doing now?"

"A little better, maybe."

I go over to the credenza next to the window where Uncle Gus's turntable and speakers sit, and I look through the albums until I find an Art Pepper with "Everything Happens to Me"—one of my favorites, and also a sort of inside joke with myself.

But when I sit down to listen the joke isn't working, which leaves just the mood, which is melancholy, and even desperate, the way Pepper plays it—those painful squawks and squeals—and after a bit I get up again and turn it off.

"No good, huh?"

"Not quite."

"How about something to eat?"

"Worth a try."

We head for the kitchen, Becky still sipping her coffee. I rinse my mug out, open the fridge and take a look inside. And right in front of my face on the top shelf is a six-pack of Woodchuck Hard Cider. Immediately my little devil starts whispering about how cider is practically apple juice and really nothing to worry about—in fact, might possibly be a drink that I could use to calm my frazzled nerves without any lasting problem! (I know this is bullshit, but I listen anyway.)

"Anything good?" Becky asks.

"Nah." I shut the door, lean against it with my arms crossed.

There's a sudden fierce battle raging inside me now, a really tough one, all the meanies pushing me toward drinking, and I wonder if it shows on my face.

"How about a couple of Italians?" I say. "I'll buy if you fly."

"Italians, huh?" She's looking at my eyes.

"Blackstone's still sells them, I imagine."

"You couldn't find anything in there?"

"Nothing exciting."

She reaches for the door handle and pulls gently until I move aside. She looks in, then back at me, and I laugh like a kid with his hand in the cookie jar.

"Woodchuck Cider? You must be pretty desperate."

"It's not that bad, actually."

She shuts the door.

"I was just tempting myself."

"Yeah, I know how that works."

I lean back against the counter.

She wanders toward the door and looks out. It's still odd to see her moving so well and standing so tall.

"So tell me something," she says. "Am I just being foolish again?"

"What do you mean?"

"Getting mixed up with you."

"Are we mixed up?"

"We seem to be."

"Well, I don't think it's foolish."

"I mean, I'm not your mother."

"Thank God for that."

"Or anything else."

She takes her pocketbook off the doorknob and slings it over her shoulder—a preparatory move. She's looking out the window again, and I'm not sure what I want. It would be a huge relief to knock down a couple of those ciders. I've come all this way, and if it could help me just get some sleep; but I know I can't do it in front of her.

Becky's not sure either. I can see it in her profile.

She shifts her weight restlessly, and for a moment I think she's as good as gone. I'm hoping for it, actually, and I wait expectantly for her to turn the doorknob and leave. I'm already rationalizing: If she'd only stayed, I would have been all right.

But then she turns and scowls at me, and instead of leaving, she walks back to the table and puts her pocketbook down.

"All right," she says. "It's true that I'm not your mother, or anything else, but you're still Julie's brother."

At first I'm disappointed. Crushed, even. But then my little drink-devil slinks off, muttering darkly, and I climb back from that pit he wanted to lead me to.

"Good," I say. "Thank you."

"So let's get rid of this stuff."

We open the bottles and dump them into the sink, and the smell of cider fills the room. She rinses the last bottle out, sets it on the counter, and says, "Just so you know, you can still tell me to leave if you want to."

I shake my head. "Nope."

"Then I'll take one of the bedrooms."

"What about work?"

"Tomorrow's Sunday."

I'm surprised to hear it. I've lost track.

She points at me. "But don't get any ideas."

"I won't."

"I'm not foolish *that* way anymore."

"You never were."

"Right." She rolls her eyes. "So are you really hungry?"

"Maybe a little."

She looks in the cupboard, finds some stale bread and peanut butter and jelly. We load up a couple of PBJs and take them back to the other room and turn on the television.

I give Becky the remote and she goes through the channels. We try a couple of sitcoms, but neither is any good, and about ten minutes into the second one she says, "The heck with this, let's walk down to the river."

"Good idea."

She shuts the TV off and we head for the door.

"Your cane?"

"I seem to be doing all right."

We cross the road and follow a path down to the riverbank. She is moving well. It really is a kind of miracle, and I hear something— an augmented chord, then another. They sound again and fade and resolve, taking on Becky's new, upright shape.

"Cool," I say.

"What's that?"

"I'll show you later."

We walk along another path through the marsh grass to the old stone pier. Downriver there are gulls circling and squawking over something I can't see.

"Scene of the crime, remember?"

"How could I forget?"

We sit on the big granite slabs, facing the river. The rock is still warm from the sun. I think it must be near high tide, as the darkening river is wide, with no mudflats left to speak of.

"Thanks for doing this, Beck."

"Don't mention it."

"It's a good thing."

"It's good and it's bad."

"What do you mean?"

"Oh, I don't know." She looks out at the river.

I ponder her strong profile and remember when we were first together, how she would catch me studying her face—I was memorizing it for later—and it would make her laugh and she'd throw a headlock on me, and we would wrestle until it turned into an embrace. And I realize I wouldn't mind that happening again. Then I tell myself I'm an idiot, and to take my mind off it, I fish my cigarettes out.

"Want one?"

"Oh, I quit a hundred years ago."

"Good for you."

I fire it up and blow smoke toward the river. We sit watching the silvery water and the gulls until I've smoked it down and then I rub it out against the granite and drop the butt into a crack between two of the big slabs, where there are still flattened old beer cans.

It's full twilight when we get back to the house.

I take her down to the basement and play the augmented chords that had come to me at the river, and she says, "What's that?"

"Do you like it?"

"Yes. It's kind of shivery."

"I heard it down by the river."

"I always liked it when you heard things like that."

I don't tell her it's about her.

We dig Uncle Gus's cribbage board out and play like old times. She's ten games ahead—some things never change—by the time she yawns and decides it's time to wrap it up and call it a night. I tap the deck of cards on the table and put the elastic back around them and put everything away.

The two bedrooms are next to each other at one end of the house, and I insist Becky take the guest room, because the bed hasn't been used.

"Don't worry, I intend to."

"Good. Sleep tight."

"Don't let the bluenotes bite."

I laugh, and she smirks and goes into the room.

I take a quilt out of Uncle Gus's closet and lie down on top of the blankets in the unmade bed. But I don't fall asleep. My brain's still tender, and I can feel Uncle Gus in this room—his Committee is in the closet—and I can't help picturing him on the floor. I think about him living here alone, and it strikes me how lonely he must have been at times, after his last student of the day left, my father gone, and access to our family shut off by Pike.

I think I could have been a better friend to him, and my old lurkers start to creep out again, and then they turn my mind toward home, and I think about being back there with Julie's ghost swooping around, and my father's ghost, too, and my mother not knowing what to make of me. And Pike, of course; no doubt he'll stick his nose into the picture somehow.

It all starts to pile up on me again.

I pull the quilt up over my head, but my little on-call demon finds me anyway and starts whispering his bullshit, and it's really hard not to listen, and the next thing I know I'm throwing back the quilt and tiptoeing to the doorway.

I look down the hallway to the kitchen, where I know if I search hard enough I'll find another stash of cider or an old bottle of Jim Beam—*something*—and I pretend I'm just tempting myself and that at any moment now I'll laugh and go back to bed.

But the longer I stand there the weaker I get.

My devil is whispering that it's a special circumstance, this return home, and just because I have a touch of whatever to calm my nerves now doesn't mean I can't get right back on the wagon after all this is over. After all, haven't I proven to myself that I can do it?

This tack gets to me, and I actually take a step into the hallway.

But then Becky opens the guest bedroom door.

She's wearing just the vocational school T-shirt, as far as I can tell—it hangs down below her hips—and in the soft light from the kitchen she looks a lot like she did twenty years before: broad-featured and strong, and with that cascade of hair, like a handsome Irish warrior-girl. Only she's standing straight, like a soldier, not knock-kneed and crooked.

"Hey," she says.

"Hi, Beck."

"You were making that noise again."

"I was? Did I wake you?"

"I wasn't asleep. So what are you up to?"

"No good, I think."

"Me?" she says. "Or the kitchen?"

"The kitchen."

"That's not very flattering."

"I figured you were out of the question."

She doesn't laugh, just looks steadily at me. Then she moves suddenly close and puts her arms around my neck. My own go automatically around her waist, and we hang together there between the two doors.

"This feels pretty normal," she says.

"It kind of does."

"I told you I was foolish."

"You're not."

"Just look at me, though."

"You haven't done anything."

"I might, though. I might at any time. Because I'm foolish, right? Unless you stop me, like I just stopped you. What about that, Cal? Are you going to stop me?"

Somehow I'm moving backwards. "I might."

"Go ahead, then."

We keep moving into the room, and then the back of my knees bump the bed, and she says, "Stop me, Cal," and when I merely tighten my arms around her, she gives me one last push.

THIRTY-FIVE

Baxter, 1995

When I wake up Becky is sitting cross-legged at the foot of the bed. She's gathered all that hair over one shoulder and is hanging onto it with both hands. And maybe she doesn't look seventeen like she did last night, but she still looks very good, especially in just the long T-shirt.

"Good morning," she says.

"You're up early."

"Never mind that."

"All right. Do I have to get up, too?"

"No. How are you feeling?"

I take a quick mental inventory, and find the lurkers and meanies seem to have gone back underground.

"Pretty good."

"Good, because I need to ask you something."

I get up on one elbow. "Go ahead."

"Did you think this was going to happen?"

"Are you kidding?"

"You couldn't tell that I was still foolish?"

"You're not foolish."

"Foolish enough to trick."

"But you're the one who started it!"

"That was the trick!"

"You lost me, Beck."

She throws her hair back over her shoulder and leans forward, elbows on her knees.

"The trick was getting me to warm up to you all over again, and knowing I'd be dumb enough to start something."

"How could I possibly do that?"

"By being nice. By making me laugh. By keeping your distance. By being tenderhearted. By playing the trumpet." She stares at my eyes.

"It's a cornet."

She looks fierce, like she might punch me.

"Sorry."

"I'm not kidding around."

"All right. But I told you plenty of bad stuff."

"You mean, like, drinking?"

"For starters."

"That was to appeal to my maternal instincts."

When I grin she looks fierce again, and I flop forward onto my stomach and take her hands. "Listen, I thought *I* was being foolish."

"Swear to God?"

"Cross my tender heart."

She stares hard, and I can see the wheels turning. Then she tucks her legs under and dives on me, putting me in the Becky headlock, and we wrestle on the bed until I break free, and then we fall onto our backs, breathing hard, looking up at the ceiling.

"So what now?"

"Maybe just see what happens?"

"If you break my heart again I'll kill you."

"I'll keep that in mind."

We turn together, smiling, our faces nearly touching. She kisses me and says, "Do you want me to come with you today?"

"Yes."

"When do you want to head over?"

I kiss her back. "Not right this second."

THIRTY-SIX

Baxter, 1995

So I'm not alone, arriving at the old farmstead two hours later. Becky O'Dell's driving, and I'm in the passenger seat, trying not to make that anxious noise. Succeeding, too; it's easier after last night, and with the two of us now. I can lean on her, because she knows where all the ghosts are.

Which isn't to say I'm not plenty nervous.

We turn in at the mailbox and I notice the old vegetable stand is gone. There are rosebushes instead, but from the way they look, no one's been tending them; they're bedraggled and there aren't many blossoms.

Becky heads up the driveway, slowly. The barn's been painted lately; it's a deeper red than before. There's a black pickup parked in front of the house.

Becky says, "Are you ready?"

"As I'll ever be."

"Good."

She drives up behind the pickup.

We get out and look at each other over the hood, she tips her head toward the house, and we circle the black pickup and climb the five steps to the porch.

I look around at the barn, the apple trees, the field leading down to the river. Then I pull the screen door open and knock on the main door.

After a minute Becky says, "Try a little more volume."

I give it a couple of healthy raps. But still nothing. I walk over to the kitchen window and shade my eyes to peer in. It looks like the same old kitchen.

"Nobody's home."

"Maybe they're at church?"

I look at my watch. "I keep forgetting it's Sunday."

"Should we wait?"

"Guess we'd better."

On the way back to her pickup I say, "Let's wait in the barn," and I grab Uncle Gus's Committee out of the extended cab on the way by. (My plan has been to find a chance to play "Blue Summer" for Julie, hoping that in her presence I can make it all the way to the end.)

We cut across to the side door, which has the same old hasp latch with a rusty screwdriver holding it shut. I pull the screwdriver out and we go in past the stalls to the drive bay. I look up at the hayloft and the timbers that run over to the hay door.

"Are you all right?"

"I think so."

There's a new boat parked where Dad's used to be, a sleek-looking sixteen-footer. (But it's still dirty.) I walk out into the bay and look up at the hayloft again. I look down at the trumpet, flutter the valves.

"Play that one from the hospital."

"It was for Julie anyway."

"It's pretty, like her."

I lean back against the double doors and put a foot up behind me and play, pointing the Committee up at the hayloft. I play "Blue Summer" up to the little sidestep, and when I move into the new part I feel it settling into a direction and a shape: I see Julie sitting on a bale of hay, and then stepping onto the parallel timbers, and starting across. I'm still playing, and I see her open the hay door and the breeze moves her hair and then swirls down and into me and out through the horn, and then I see her sitting on the left-hand beam and telling me to turn around.

I stop and lower the horn.

"What is it?" Becky says.

"I just remembered something."

I hand her the horn and walk over to the ladder affixed to the beam and test the rungs. It feels pretty solid, so I start climbing. There's no scurrying above me, and I think Pike must have finally starved those cats out: great victory for the Big Man.

I keep climbing, putting one foot after the other, and then I'm at the top rung and pushing myself over. I roll away from the edge and stand up.

"Cal? What's going on?"

"Tell you in a minute."

I walk over to the conveyor timbers, feeling ahead with my toes before each step in case there's a rotten board hidden beneath the loose hay. I look over the edge at Becky and my stomach turns over on itself. You always hear that distances and heights are smaller than you remember, but this still looks pretty high to me.

"You're not going across."

"I think I might be."

"Not sure that's a good idea."

"That makes two of us."

"Why don't I hunt up a ladder?"

"No, I have to do this."

A ladder would make more sense, but it's not what I want. I have to go over because of what I remembered, and I have to do it the way I couldn't then. It's almost a musical feeling, like my life has been a complex chord, and this is how it might finally resolve.

I'm not dumb enough to try and walk the beams, though. Instead I sit down and ease myself onto the right-hand timber. Then I start hunching across.

"You're scaring me, Cal."

"I can't talk right now."

I work my way very carefully out onto the timber. It creaks once and I freeze, trying not to panic, and when nothing happens I start moving again. When I get out in the middle it feels very precarious, and I nearly freeze again, but I know if I do, I might be stuck, and the fear pushes me forward.

I make it across out of sheer momentum. Then all I can do at first is hook my hand under the nailed board and hold on.

When I can breathe again I slip my other hand behind the lower board and fish out a little spiral notebook with a stub of pencil stuck into the wire binding.

"I knew it," I say.

"What is it?"

"I'll have to show you."

I reach behind and fit it into my hip pocket. Then I turn very carefully and start back.

"Easy does it," Becky says from below.

"Don't worry about that."

But on the way back things start batting around, shapes diving on me from all over the barn, trying to knock me loose. I try to push through like I did going over, and I keep going as long as I can, but then it gets so bad that I have to stop. I'm only about ten feet from the platform, too. But I just can't move.

I let myself down onto the timber and hold on tight.

"Are you all right?"

"I just need a minute."

I press my cheek against the timber and wait for it to ease, but the bombardment continues until I want to let go and slip over sideways just to make it stop. But I can't let that happen because I have to read Julie's notebook.

Then I hear movement, and Becky quietly saying, "Hey."

I open my eyes, and she's standing on the platform.

"How'd you get up here?"

"I flew up on my broomstick."

This makes me laugh despite everything.

"Come on back now."

"Not sure I can, Beck."

"You can, or I'm coming out."

She sits, legs hanging down on either side of the same timber I'm on. When I don't move she puts her hands on the edge of the platform and hops forward a couple of inches onto the timber.

The timber creaks again, and I say, "All right!" and push myself up, my hands flat on the wood. I feel very shaky, like I might have some kind of spasm.

But Becky says, "Keep looking at me," and I do, and when she says, "Come on, now," I lean forward and move my hands and inch or so. Then I hunch myself toward her.

"Do it again."

I do it again, and once more, and then I'm moving steadily along, and I feel Julie with me. She's smiling and she's come out of the rafters to ride along for the last couple of feet.

"Why didn't you do that sooner?" I say.

"What?" Becky says,

"Nothing." I didn't realize I was talking out loud.

Becky lifts herself backward off the beam and onto the platform as I get closer, and when I'm within reach, she takes my hand and leans away, pulling hard, feet braced against the edge, and then I'm rolling with Julie and Becky onto the platform and we're all tumbling backwards into the hay bales, and it's as if no time and all time has passed since we were together.

THIRTY-SEVEN

Baxter, 1995

It's too dim in the barn to read, so we go out the side door and sit on the old half-log bench in the bright sunshine.

There are only a dozen or so pages of writing in the notebook. The first one says PRIVATE—DO NOT ENTER! and PROPERTY OF JULIA MARY SHAW. Then it explains how "a person whose name I refuse to utter" discovered the diary she'd hidden in her room and read everything about how much she hated him. She was in big trouble, now. He still wasn't going to keep her from writing everything down, though, because this one would stay up by the hay door, where he was too fat to go, and where I couldn't get to it, either, because she had to make sure I didn't know what was going on or I'd be in big trouble too.

It gets so bad that I can hardly make out the words. But Julie's still here, and she won't let me look away. So I read everything about the bullying, the harassment, the outright abuse that happened after Pike found the original diary. I hear Julie describing the daily humiliations, some of which I saw but was too scared to do anything about.

By the time I close the book I want to throw up.

It's all there, and I realize I'd always known, deep down, how bad it got.

I hand Becky the notebook and wait.

After a little while I hear her gasp and I know she's reading about Pike's lectures in Julie's room, with her face between hands and his nose touching hers; she's reading about the grabbing and shaking, and "Keep it up, Princess, and see what happens."

And worst of all, the spankings, with Julie pinned across his lap while he "taught her a little respect," at first by the book, and then, more uncomfortable, and finally with her panties all the way down, and Julie "feeling him under there" while he slapped her bare bottom, which made her so sick she threw up on the floor.

Julie's still narrating in my head, and I admire her composure, her grace, as she tells me how he stood over her while she cleaned it up and told her that if she said a word to anyone, there'd be hell to pay—and this especially meant her mouthy little brother, unless she wanted his wagon fixed for good.

That's the last entry, which she must have written that day on the beams while I had my back to her.

"Oh my God," Becky says.

"The son of a bitch."

"She never said anything."

"She was scared."

Becky is silent for a moment.

I feel Julie still with us, glad I made it back. I feel her elegance and coolness—she seems all grown up—and I'm glad I made it back, too.

"Foss needs to see this," Becky says.

"Damn right."

She hands me back the notebook, and I stick it in my pocket. I pick up the Committee and we start back to the Silverado.

There's a lot going on in my head, bad, dismal stuff trying to take over, but it's not at its best; it's fitful and pale, and then there's a countercharge that comes from all of us: me, Julie, and Becky, too. There's a pure, strong mingling of smooth-edged shapes and colors and harmony—sevenths—that is coming *from* us, not *at* us, and we all turn together to face the light green minivan turning off the River Road, and Becky says "That's Alvin's," and it all coalesces into something complete, something proud and dark.

The minivan comes up the driveway and parks behind the Silverado.

Pike, my mother, Alvin and his wife and two kids get out and walk toward us in their church clothes.

My mother looks like a sixty-year-old woman, one I barely know.

Alvin's not skinny anymore, and his wife is pretty.

"The Prodigal Son!" Alvin says, grinning.

Then he's talking, and my mother's trying to say something and Alvin's wife and kids are staring, but all I'm really aware of is Pike lumbering into range with a smirk he's not quite trying to hide.

He looks pretty much the same, with a bigger gut and some gray in his crew cut, and then he's close and his smirk turns into one of the old meat-eater grins, and I suddenly see him with Julie, naked, across his lap, his hand in the air, and I feel Julie still with me, and she's waiting.

She's been waiting.

Pike stops next to my mother.

"Cal, are you all right?" Alvin peers at me, as if he can detect some of the notes going off in my head.

Becky puts a hand on my arm, and then that proud, dark shape in my head—the blend of my fury, Julie's fierce dignity, and Becky's outrage—focuses and narrows, and I hear the "Blue Summer" melody, the ending I've needed, and there's a last dark complex chord, and I'm lifting my trumpet as if to play it when something happens and suddenly Pike is down on the gravel, blood pooling in the dirt by his ear, and my mother is kneeling beside him, everybody else is yelling.

Becky's staring at the Committee.

There's blood smeared on the hard bottoms of the valves. I look back at Pike and then I sit down on the porch steps. I need to wait for things to clear up. Seems like somehow I've always been sitting on this porch, waiting. But this time, it's so noisy.

Alvin runs past me into the house, and Pike is still down and not moving.

Becky sits beside me and slips the little notebook out of my back pocket.

I'm not sure how long we sit there. But pretty soon, all kinds of sirens are coming down the River Road. There are flashing blue and red lights, and both town cruisers turn up the driveway, followed by the ambulance.

Becky stands up and walks out to meet them.

Bolduc Correctional Facility, 1997

So here we are, and that's the story behind all those lurid headlines.

I was charged with manslaughter, but because of Julie's notebook the prosecutor made it a class C felony, which is a maximum of five years instead of thirty, and the judge put me in the Bolduc Correctional Facility instead of the Maine State Prison. (This was big, because the only musical instruments they allow in the Maine State Prison are guitars and harmonicas, neither of which I can play.)

So I get to keep my horns in my room.

I say horns because I inherited Uncle Gus's Committee. He passed away that same year without ever fully regaining consciousness, which means I never got to talk to him again. (Which is a shame, because there's a lot I would have liked to say.)

It's good to have two horns, because that way I get to swap off, which keeps me fresh as far as playing something new. There's also a piano in the Bolduc that I can use to compose. In case you wondered about the section headings in this book, they're all the names of songs I've created, some of which have been published. These songs have been coming at me from all directions, and I've had to work hard to keep up. I'm not sure if that works in a literary way, but they all seemed to derive from this story as I told it, and weren't to be excluded.

I also inherited Uncle G's house. Becky's living there now, and I'll join her when I get out, which should be in another seven months or so, because of what they call "good time" here, which is the same as time off for good behavior.

I think our first visitors might be Loretta McCarty and Georgie. She wrote to me after seeing one of the news reports, and we've corresponded ever since. In fact, my letters to her were the start of this book. See, once I got started writing about it I couldn't stop. I guess it was therapeutic.

You're probably wondering how I feel about it now.

It's complicated, but I guess I think that Pike got what was coming to him. There's still a lurking horror that I took a life, and I'll have to live with that. But I've settled on the idea that it was retribution delivered through me—not *by* me, or I'd remember it, which I still don't.

I think the retribution came from Julie, which is good enough for me.

Rationalization, maybe. But there it is.

Neither my unfathomable mother nor Alvin has tried to come in to see me. I guess it's complicated for them, too. It must have been terrible to witness, and maybe they don't believe everything Julie wrote in her notebook. Or maybe they do, and can't admit it to themselves, which would be more in keeping with the past, right?

Anyway, that's my story, as well as I can tell it. Probably as a writer I'm a pretty good musician, but I hope I haven't ranged too far afield along the way. I've just been going where the shape of it leads me, following the notes, playing the melody, playing the riffs when it's my turn to swing, trying to follow where it wants me to go.

Acknowledgments

My deepest appreciation to the amazing crew at Islandport Press: Dean Lunt, Teresa Lagrange, Holly Eddy, Shannon Butler and Taylor McCafferty, with special thanks to my brilliant editor, Genevieve Morgan; and to Melissa Hayes.